MODERN
NATIONS
—OF THE—
WORLD

NICARAGUA

TITLES IN THE MODERN NATIONS OF THE WORLD SERIES INCLUDE:

Afghanistan	Kenya
Algeria	Kuwait
Argentina	Lebanon
Australia	Liberia
Austria	Libya
Belize	Mexico
Bolivia	Morocco
Brazil	Nigeria
Cambodia	North Korea
Canada	Norway
Chile	Pakistan
China	Panama
Colombia	Peru
Congo	Philippines
Costa Rica	Poland
Cuba	Russia
Czech Republic	Saudi Arabia
Denmark	Scotland
Egypt	Sri Lanka
England	Somalia
Ethiopia	South Africa
Finland	South Korea
France	Spain
Germany	Sudan
Greece	Sweden
Guatemala	Switzerland
Haiti	Syria
Hungary	Taiwan
India	Thailand
Indonesia	Turkey
Iran	United Arab Emirates
Iraq	United States
Ireland	Vatican City
Israel	Vietnam
Italy	Yemen
Japan	
Jordan	

NICARAGUA

BY DEBRA A. MILLER

LUCENT BOOKS

An imprint of Thomson Gale, a part of The Thomson Corporation

THOMSON
™
GALE

Detroit • New York • San Francisco • San Diego • New Haven, Conn. • Waterville, Maine • London • Munich

On cover: This rooftop view shows colorful León,
one of Nicaragua's oldest cities.

LIBRARY OF CONGRESS CATALOGING-IN-PUBLICATION DATA

Miller, Debra A.
  Nicaragua / by Debra A. Miller.
    p. cm. — (Modern nations of the world)
  Includes bibliographical references and index.
  ISBN 1-59018-731-8 (hardcover : alk. paper)
  1. Nicaragua—Juvenile literature. I. Title. II. Series.
F1523.2.M55 2005
972.85—dc22
                                                          2005001799

Printed in the United States of America

Contents

INTRODUCTION

A DIFFICULT ROAD

Nicaragua, a country located in the middle of Central America, has had a very turbulent history. Nicaraguans have had to live through foreign interventions, civil wars, dictatorships, natural disasters, political corruption, and poverty. Nicaragua's difficult saga began when its Pacific coast, along with much of the rest of Central America, was conquered and settled as a Spanish colony in the early sixteenth century. Spanish rule decimated the indigenous population and imposed a Hispanic culture on the area. At the same time, the British occupied the eastern coast of Nicaragua, posing a challenge to Spanish rule and dividing the region into two opposing cultures. The Central American colonies, including Nicaragua, declared their independence from Spain in 1821, and Nicaragua became a republic independent of the United Provinces of Central America in 1838.

Independence from Spain, however, did not bring true freedom for Nicaraguans. Instead, Nicaragua continued to be dominated by Britain and later the United States. These countries largely controlled both Nicaragua's economy and its internal politics for many decades. In the mid-1800s, Nicaragua was even taken over by a U.S. citizen for a short period, and U.S. marines were stationed in the country for much of the early twentieth century. Although U.S. troops were eventually forced out in 1933, the United States thereafter continued its influence through its support of Anastasio Somoza. Somoza, his family, and friends ruled Nicaragua for more than forty years. While in power, the Somozas stole much of the country's wealth for their own personal use and placed Nicaragua deep into foreign debt. Nicaraguans finally rose up against the dictatorship in 1979, bringing a new revolutionary Sandinista government into power.

Yet the road has remained difficult for Nicaraguans. Even after their revolution, civil war continued. Because the Sandinistas embraced Socialist ideas and provided aid to leftist rebels in neighboring El Salvador, the United States in the 1980s cut off aid and trade to Nicaragua and sponsored a rebel group, called the Contras, who opposed the new Nicaraguan government. This Contra war, coming on the heels of Nicaragua's previous struggle with dictatorship and dependency, damaged the country's economy and caused greater poverty among the population. The Sandinistas were defeated in the 1990 elections, but some succeeding government administrations have been ineffective and riddled with corruption, further testing the hope and endurance of the Nicaraguan people.

Adding to the country's challenges throughout its history have been natural disasters, including earthquakes, volcanic eruptions, and strong hurricanes that have caused

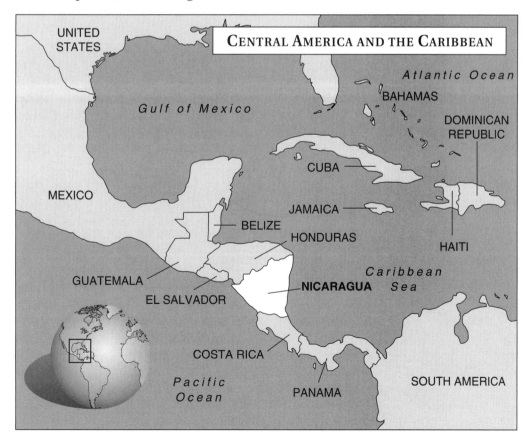

substantial deaths, homelessness, and destruction among an already traumatized people. An earthquake and volcanic eruption in 1972, for example, destroyed Managua, Nicaragua's capital city. Hurricane Joan wreaked havoc on the country in 1988 and a decade later, in 1998, Nicaragua was hard hit by an even more massive storm, Hurricane Mitch. These disasters killed and injured thousands, destroyed roads and property, and left large numbers of the population homeless and poorer than they were before. After each disaster, the government, beset with a weak economy and insufficient revenues, was overwhelmed and unable to respond or rebuild without international aid.

Today, Nicaragua remains one of the Western Hemisphere's poorest countries. Nicaraguans continue to face ex-

Sandinista soldiers raise their weapons in celebration during a 1984 rally in Managua. The Sandinistas seized power in 1979, promising sweeping political and social change.

treme poverty, widespread unemployment, and a huge foreign debt. Moreover, international aid to the country in recent years has come with strings attached, requiring
Nicaragua to reduce government spending at a time when
social programs such as education and health care are desperately needed by its people. Although the country has
made progress toward economic stability over the past few
years, economic growth is still far too slow to meet the country's needs. It therefore seems certain that Nicaragua will
continue to be dependent on international aid and influence
for the near future.

Despite these many challenges, however, observers report
that Nicaraguans seem grateful to be finally free and generally hopeful about their future. Most struggle to find whatever work they can to feed themselves and their children,
and eagerly embrace any opportunity for education or improvement in their lives. Many also worry about corruption
in their government and long for more ethical leaders who
can lead Nicaragua toward greater openness and prosperity.
Nicaragua's past journey has been troubled; perhaps its future course will be a smoother one.

1

UNTOUCHED BEAUTY

Nicaragua lies in the heart of Central America, the narrow isthmus of land that connects North and South America. It is bordered by Honduras to the north, Costa Rica to the south, the Caribbean Sea to the east, and the Pacific Ocean to the west. Although Nicaragua is the largest country in Central America, it is still quite small. It occupies only 49,998 square miles (129,494 sq. km), a territory roughly the size of New York State. Yet despite its relative smallness, Nicaragua is blessed with a variety of climates and geographical features, and an abundance of forests, wildlife, and plants. In addition, Nicaragua's political difficulties have slowed the rate of economic development in the country, leaving much of the country's great natural beauty and resources still untouched.

THE PACIFIC COASTAL PLAIN

Nicaragua's geography can be divided into three geographical zones: the Pacific coastal plain, the central highlands, and the Caribbean lowlands. The Pacific region features a narrow, flat area that extends about 50 miles (80.5km) inland from the western coast. Some of this land is covered in natural grasslands that turn green during the rainy season but remain dry and brown the rest of the year. Large parts of the area known as the Pacific plain, however, are not really flat at all but are instead made up of fertile rolling hills, many of them planted in coffee trees.

The coastal plain is divided in two by a long string of more than forty volcanoes. The volcanoes run north to south from the country's northern border to a point south of Lake Managua, a large lake located in the central part of the Pacific region. A few volcanoes can also be found as far south as Lake Nicaragua, an enormous freshwater lake in the southern part of the Pacific region. Most of Nicaragua's volcanoes are dormant, but many are active volcanoes, which means they occasionally erupt and spew steam, smoke, ash, and lava over the countryside. The volcano cones rise high above the surrounding valleys and are the most striking aspect of the Nicaraguan landscape. As travel writer Paul Glassman notes, "Wherever you go in the heartland of Nicaragua, you will be within sight of some evidence of the periodically irascible [early angered] innards of the earth, whether steaming, fuming, or belching fire and ash and lava and boulders."[1] The volcanic areas are also the site of earthquakes, another common geological feature in Nicaragua.

The volcanic soil in the Pacific lowlands produces rich farmland that has made the region famous for its agriculture. In fact, this area is considered the breadbasket of Nicaragua, the place where most of its crops are grown and its livestock raised. This region is also the most densely populated part of Nicaragua. The country's capital city of Managua is located here, as are most of the nation's other significant urban centers and most of the country's major highways.

THE CENTRAL HIGHLANDS

Northeast of the Pacific region are the central highlands, a triangle-shaped area composed of rugged mountain ranges,

VOLCANOES, EARTHQUAKES, AND HURRICANES

Nicaragua's geography and location make it vulnerable to some of the most destructive forces in nature. Nicaraguans have always lived next to a string of volcanoes located on the western side of the country. Most of these volcanoes lie dormant, but a number have periodically erupted, sending ash, lava, and boulders into nearby farms, villages, and cities. An eruption by La Concepción volcano in the 1960s, for example, destroyed many farms lying at its base. The city of León, situated near the active Cerro Negro volcano, is often choked by clouds of volcanic ash. Eventually, however, the ash improves the fertility of the soil, making it rich in organic matter and minerals.

The forces of nature that produce volcanoes also produce numerous earthquakes in Nicaragua. Most are minor, but a massive earthquake in 1972 destroyed the capital city of Managua. Perhaps the biggest natural threat to Nicaragua, however, is hurricanes. The rains and high winds of Hurricane Joan in 1988 killed 432 people, left 180,000 homeless, and caused $1 billion in

property damage. A few years later, in 1998, Hurricane Mitch destroyed over $1 billion of property, left 800,000 homeless, and killed over 3,000 people.

In 1955 plumes of ash and smoke spew from Cerro Negro, a volcano near the city of León.

deep valleys, and major rivers that drain toward Nicaragua's western lakes or eastward to the Caribbean. The western side of these mountains is relatively dry with few rivers or streams; on the eastern, Caribbean-side slopes, however, are numerous rivers and much wetter conditions. Rainfall in this eastern region, in fact, can vary between 70 and 100 inches (178 to 254cm) per year, creating an extremely humid climate.

Because of the rain and high humidity, most of the mountains in the eastern part of the central highlands are covered with cloud rain forests, forests that grow in the mist at altitudes above about 3,000 feet (914m). In these forests, towering hardwoods such as oak, walnut, Spanish cedar, and a few mahogany trees flourish, covered by lush Spanish moss, delicate orchids, and a tangle of vines. Toward the country's northern border, however, the rain forests give way to pine forests, sometimes mixed with oak. On the highest mountains, tropical fir trees can be found.

Most of these mountain ridges run east to west, and some rise more than 6,000 feet (1,829m) above sea level. The tallest mountain in Nicaragua, Mogotón Peak, for example, is located far north, close to the Honduran border, and stands at 6,912 feet (2,107m). Farther south, the mountains tend to be smaller, many rising only to about 3,000 feet (914m) in height. These areas are perfect for coffee cultivation. The coffee plants grow under the shade of trees, such as banana, fig, and avocado trees. Except for the coffee farms, this part of Nicaragua is sparsely populated. As political scientist David Close explains:

> In many ways the Central Highlands are still a pioneer region where subsistence agriculture is the rule. Outside the few important towns, . . . communications are poor, education and health services badly underdeveloped, and little of the infrastructure needed for a modern economy is in place.[2]

THE CARIBBEAN LOWLANDS

On the eastern side of the country, the Caribbean lowlands form Nicaragua's largest territory—a long, hot, and exceedingly humid coastal plain. Occupying more than 50 percent of Nicaragua's total territory, this area is also called the

A Miskito Indian girl runs down a dirt road in her village on the Mosquito Coast, an area of Nicaragua that receives an average of 100 to 250 inches (254 to 635cm) of rain each year.

Mosquito Coast, named after an indigenous group called the Mosquitos (today, the Miskito). This is the wettest area in Central America. It receives 100 to 250 inches (254 to 635cm) of rain each year and drains many of the large rivers and streams originating in the central mountains.

Except for floodplain areas next to the numerous rivers and streams, much of the soil here is made of sand and gravel and is not good for farming. Instead, the Caribbean coastal area is the site of broad grasslands and pine savannas, with large lowland tropical rain forests in the interior west of the savannas along rivers, and in the southern, more mountainous part of the coast. The shoreline is hot and swampy and home to mangrove trees, shallow lagoons, and stagnant salt marshes.

Because of the heat, humidity, and lack of good soil, the Caribbean coast is the least populated part of Nicaragua. As political science professor Thomas W. Walker notes, "This vast region has never been able to support a large human population—at present less than 8 percent of the national total lives there."[3] Few roads have been built in this area, and there are only two main settlements, at the coastal towns of Bluefields and Puerto Cabezas. About 55 miles (89km) east of Bluefields lie the Corn Islands, two small coral islands that have become popular with tourists and scuba divers. Separated from the rest of the country by the interior mountains, this eastern area has also developed a history and culture completely different from that of the majority population. Unlike in the western part of the country where a Hispanic culture prevails, the small population on the eastern coast is largely composed of Afro-Caribbean people and indigenous Indian tribes.

LAKES AND RIVERS

In addition to two long coasts bordering both the Pacific and the Caribbean, Nicaragua is a land with numerous freshwater lakes and rivers. The country's backbone of mountains is the source of rivers that flow both east and west. Most of the greatest rivers flow eastward toward the Caribbean. These include the Río Coco, the longest river in Central America, which flows along the border with Honduras; the Grande de Matagalpa, another long river in central eastern Nicaragua; and the mighty Escondido, a navigable river in the south that connects the town of Bluefields with the interior of Nicaragua. In the west, a few rivers, such as the Negro and the Tecolapa, flow into the Pacific Ocean in northern Nicaragua. These rivers, however, tend to be short, and they often dry up during the summers. The more important westerly rivers, such as the Viejo, Mayales, and San Antonio, flow into and help to maintain Nicaragua's two great lakes, Lake Managua and Lake Nicaragua.

These lakes are another of the country's most striking features. Lake Nicaragua is the largest freshwater lake in Central America. It measures 100 miles (161km) long and 45 miles (72km) wide and is fed by a smaller lake, Lake Managua. Lake Nicaragua is so large that from the shore it looks like the ocean; a person standing on one shore cannot see the other shore. Like an ocean, the lake also contains many islands within its waters. These islands are covered with beautiful, lush, jungle vegetation, and some have comfortable hotels for tourists. Both Lake Managua and Lake Nicaragua were formed by earthquakes, which scientists believe caused seawater to be surrounded by land and raised to an altitude of about 100 feet (31m) above sea level. A number of other lakes, many of them created in the craters of ancient volcanoes, can also be found in the western Pacific region.

Flowing out of the southern rim of Lake Nicaragua is the country's most important river, the Río San Juan. The Río San Juan runs eastward for 124 miles (200km) along the border between Nicaragua and Costa Rica; it connects Lake Nicaragua to the Caribbean Sea. Except for a few areas of rapids, the river is entirely navigable. As a result, the Río San Juan has been important economically to both Nicaragua and Costa Rica. Pirates and settlers used the river to reach inland areas during colonial times, and it continues to be a reliable commercial transit route across Central America today. At various times during Nicaragua's history, the Río San Juan has even been considered as a possible site for a transcontinental canal to link the Caribbean with the Pacific.

RAIN FORESTS, FLORA, AND FAUNA

Nicaragua's rugged geography and abundant water have produced some of the largest untouched forests in Central America. The country's relatively small population and lack of development has allowed much of this forested area to remain undisturbed. Some of these virgin forests are upland cloud rain forests, which grow at high altitudes in the mountains that point toward the Caribbean plains. Other forested areas on the western, drier side of the mountains are called dry tropical forests. The dry forests contain trees that grow and bloom during the wet season but lose their leaves to conserve energy during the dry season. Most of these dry forests have been cut down due to population growth in the west, but a few still grow on Nicaragua's southern Pacific slopes.

Perhaps the country's greatest natural treasure, however, is its lowland tropical rain forests. These pristine, evergreen rain forests cover much of central and southeastern Nicaragua. They contain dozens of tree species, including ceiba (a tall, umbrella-shaped evergreen), guanacaste (a large, common tropical evergreen), mahogany, Spanish cedar, and almond. Remarkably, many of these giant trees grow more than 100 feet (31m) high and 4 to 5 feet (1.2 to 1.5m) wide in poor, rain-leached soil and have very shallow roots. Yet they form a dense canopy that provides habitat for millions of tree-dwelling species. With the sun blocked, the forest floor stays shady and cool, and also teems with countless creatures, ranging from insects to larger jungle animals, such as jaguars and howler monkeys.

Rough estimates, for example, suggest that Nicaragua's forests are home to over eight thousand plant species, including over one thousand types of orchids alone. Ferns, vines, and shrubs are also common rain forest flora. In addition, countless numbers of animals flourish in the tropical

NICARAGUA'S LAKE SHARKS

Lake Nicaragua is home to the world's only species of freshwater shark. Experts claim that these sharks migrated to the lake many years ago by swimming up the Río San Juan, which connects Lake Nicaragua to the Caribbean Sea. The sharks adapted to the freshwater environment and survived. Scientists once believed that the sharks were a separate species that became landlocked in Lake Nicaragua. However, researchers who have studied the sharks have found that, although they can live in the freshwater lake for periods of several years, they travel back down the Río San Juan to the sea to reproduce and bear their young.

Today, the Lake Nicaragua shark (also called the bull shark) is considered the most dangerous shark in the world. It has a large body and very powerful jaws, and it will eat practically anything. It is believed to be responsible for many human deaths. Besides in Nicaragua, the species has been seen in many other parts of the world, including other freshwater environments such as the Mississippi River in the United States.

The world's only species of freshwater shark, the bull shark, lives in Lake Nicaragua.

rain forests. More than seven hundred types of birds, three hundred kinds of reptiles and amphibians, hundreds upon hundreds of mammals and fish species, and a vast array of insects have been identified here. Typical forest animals include monkeys, jaguars, deer, tapirs (a large nocturnal mammal with a long, rubbery snout), raccoons, and sloths. They share the jungle with many brightly colored birds, such as parrots, macaws, and toucans, as well as a wide variety of other bird species ranging from high-flying hawks to tiny hummingbirds to birds common to North America (such as swallows, falcons, and owls). Adding to this menagerie are numerous kinds of poisonous and nonpoisonous snakes, iguanas, and colorful lizards and frogs in various sizes.

Nicaragua's pristine tropical rain forests are home to thousands upon thousands of animal and flower species.

Elsewhere in Nicaragua, other creatures flourish. In the country's numerous rivers crocodiles and otters swim, and in Lake Nicaragua one finds many types of fish, including swordfish, shad, and the huge tarpon, a fish sought after by sports fishermen. Lake Nicaragua's most famous marine creature, however, is the bull shark, a unique type of freshwater shark. Bull sharks and many of Lake Nicaragua's fish are usually saltwater species, but scientists believe these ocean fish adapted to freshwater as Lake Nicaragua changed from a saltwater to a freshwater lake.

CLIMATE

Nicaragua's great natural bounty is largely due to its abundant rainfall and warm, tropical climate. Temperatures vary little and are influenced mostly by elevation. In lower elevations such as the coastal areas (called *tierra caliente*, or "hot land") daytime temperatures average around 82 to 90 degrees Fahrenheit (27 to 32 degrees Celsius) and can drop to around 70 degrees (21°C) at night. Throughout much of the central highlands (the *tierra templada*, or "temperate land"), temperatures range from 80 degrees (26.6°C) during the day to 60 degrees (15.5°C) at night. At higher elevations (the *tierra fría*, or "cold land") temperatures are somewhat cooler, with average temperatures in the 70s (20s Celsius) during the daytime and as low as the 50s (10s Celsius) at night.

Unlike temperatures, rainfall varies widely in Nicaragua. The eastern Caribbean lowlands receive the most rain, as much as 250 inches (635cm) per year. The Pacific side of the country, on the other hand, receives much less precipitation, as little as 39 inches (99cm) annually. The lack of rainfall in the west is caused by the peaks of the central highlands, which block the moisture-laden Caribbean trade winds from reaching the western slopes and lowlands. The rainfall in Nicaragua is also seasonal. Rains typically come between May and October, which is the rainy season, and cease for most of the rest of the year, a period known as the dry season.

During the rainy season, many of Nicaragua's eastern rivers overflow their banks, filling the wide floodplains in the Caribbean lowlands. The rainy season on the eastern coast also means hurricane season, when high winds and heavy rains frequently batter the area and sometimes even cause extensive damage inland. Much of Nicaragua was devastated, for example, by Hurricane Mitch in November 1998, when more than a year's worth of rain fell in just seven days.

CITIES AND POPULATION

Given the uncomfortable and sometimes dangerous weather in the east, it is not suprising that most Nicaraguans live in

PROTECTING THE RAIN FORESTS

Nicaragua's pristine rain forests are disappearing at the rate of 400 square miles (1,036 sq. km) per year. At this rate, there may be no forests left by the year 2025. Unfortunately, Nicaragua's government has failed to protect the rain forests. Instead, laws protecting the forests have been repeatedly broken. In 1996, for example, the government granted thirty-year logging rights for 150,000 acres (60,705 ha) of pristine rain forest to Solcarsa, part of a large South Korean corporation. Solcarsa cut down many ancient tropical hardwood trees, built a road through the forest that destroyed watersheds and habitat in the nearby national forest reserve, and displaced many indigenous people from their traditional lands. Court action successfully challenged the contract, but the government continued to allow logging until 1998, when Solcarsa withdrew from Nicaragua for financial reasons.

Today, legal and illegal logging continues in Nicaragua's forests, along with ranching and farming activities that cause rapid deforestation. As a result of the government's ineffectiveness, a number of nongovernmental organizations and environmental groups have joined the fight to preserve Nicaragua's rain forests. These groups are trying to place pressure on the Nicaraguan government and the international community to ensure that the country's precious environmental resources are not lost.

the western part of the country. Most cities and towns are located there, linked by the country's few major highways. In fact, more than 60 percent of the nation's population of over 5 million people live near the country's western urban areas, many of them in or around the growing capital city of Managua. Managua's population (including its suburbs) is estimated at around 1.4 million, making it by far the largest city in Nicaragua.

Managua is located on the shores of Lake Managua. It is an ancient city, already populated when the Spanish arrived, and since 1852 it has been the nation's capital. Managua is also part of an active seismic area; it has been damaged repeatedly by earthquakes throughout its long existence. The latest disaster occurred in 1972, when a great earthquake killed more than twenty thousand residents and leveled most of the heart of the city. Managua was eventually rebuilt and today functions as a modern city, serving as a major commercial and transportation hub and political center. Rather than rebuilding the crowded town center after the 1972 disaster, however, Nicaragua dispersed its businesses and industry, allowing the city to spread outward. As a result, the suburbs grew, creating a large urban residential area.

Nicaragua's second largest city is historic León, a relatively quiet provincial town just a short distance north of Managua with a population of about 150,000. León was first built in 1524 by the Spanish on the shores of Lake Managua, but it was moved northwest to its present location after being destroyed by an earthquake and volcanic eruption in 1609. Today it is the site of Nicaragua's most prestigious academic institution, National University, and is also known for its colonial architecture.

Other major cities in western Nicaragua include Granada and Masaya. Granada (pop. 70,000), founded about the same time as León (in 1523), is the main port on Lake Nicaragua and a leading commercial, transportation, and manufacturing center. Masaya (pop. 100,000), a city near Managua located on the extinct Masaya Volcano, serves as a transportation and commercial center for surrounding agricultural areas. It is also known for its production of local handicrafts. In the central highlands, the main settlement is Matagalpa (pop. 70,000), an important commercial center for coffee and other industries nestled in the mountains.

On the Caribbean side of the country, there are significantly fewer people but some smaller towns can be found. One is Bluefields, a tropical outpost with a population of about forty-eight thousand located on the shore of a coastal lagoon created at the mouth of the Escondido River. The town was hit with two-hundred-mile-per-hour winds in 1988 when Hurricane Joan arrived in the area, but it has been largely rebuilt and today once again features numerous clapboard houses with tin roofs and wide porches typical of the poor, laidback Caribbean lifestyle. Residents here speak English instead of Spanish, and the area seems a world away from Managua and western Nicaragua's culture. The other main Caribbean coastal town is Puerto Cabezas (also called Bilwi). With a population of about fifty-one thousand, it is located about 350 miles (563km) northwest of Bluefields and is home to several surrounding communities of Miskito, Rama, and Sumu Indians. Puerto Cabezas functions largely as a fishing port for lobster, shrimp, and prawns.

Thanks to this sparse population in the eastern Caribbean region, as well as the limitations placed on economic development as a result of the country's political difficulties, Nicaragua today is blessed with many virtually untouched natural treasures. If these environmental riches can be preserved and protected, some experts think they may one day provide a key to the country's future prosperity.

Nicaragua's capital city of Managua sits on the shores of Lake Managua. The city serves as the country's commercial and transportation hub.

NICARAGUA'S EARLY DAYS

Nicaragua's early history was similar to that of other Central American nations: Indigenous Nicaraguans were conquered by the Spanish, who ruled as a colonial power for three hundred years. After gaining independence from Spain, Nicaraguans hoped for full independence but instead faced years of foreign intervention, leading to a long period of repressive, dictatorial rule. Democracy and true independence came very late for Nicaragua.

EARLY INHABITANTS

Since its early history Nicaragua has been home to two distinct cultures—a Hispanic culture that developed in the west due to Aztec and Spanish influences and a completely different British/Caribbean culture in the eastern part of the country.

The fertile Pacific plains in western Nicaragua have long attracted settlers. The earliest known inhabitants of Nicaragua lived near Lake Nicaragua and Lake Managua around ten thousand years ago. Archaeologists know this because of ten-thousand-year-old footprints that were preserved under layers of volcanic ash near Lake Managua. The footprints were made by people and animals fleeing an ancient volcanic eruption. Other evidence shows that western Nicaragua's earliest indigenous people may have migrated to the area from Mexico. Experts say they spoke a language similar to that of the early Aztec and Mayan cultures of Mexico. Eventually, these people formed stable settlements where they cultivated crops such as corn, beans, chili peppers, avocados, and squash.

By the early 1500s, western Nicaragua was inhabited by over a million people, who formed three main tribes—the Niquirano, the Chorotegano, and the Chontal. The Niquirano people lived in large agricultural settlements around Lake Managua and Lake Nicaragua. They were governed by caciques, or chieftains. The Chorotegano lived nearby but farther inland. The Chontal tribes lived in the central highlands region. These tribes frequently warred with each other and did not develop the sophisticated cities and civilization associated with nearby indigenous peoples such as the Mayans.

The Caribbean side of the country, meanwhile, became home to other tribes that are believed to have migrated from what is today Colombia, a country in South America. These eastern Nicaraguans survived by hunting, fishing, and slash-and-burn agriculture. They moved from place to place as soils became depleted, and some traded with, intermarried, and adopted the culture of black Caribbean slaves who fled to Nicaragua from Britain's Caribbean settlements. This mixed indigenous/Caribbean group became known as the Miskito and eventually pushed other, smaller indigenous

An archaeologist unearths pottery from an ancient Niquirano burial site near Lake Managua. The cemetery contained the graves of about twenty people.

groups south and farther into the interior of Nicaragua.
These other indigenous tribes were called the Sumu and
Rama.

A SPANISH COLONY

Nicaragua was first explored by Spain in 1502 when Christopher Columbus arrived on the Caribbean side of the country. It was not until 1522, however, that the Spanish, hoping
to exploit the raw materials
of the area, explored the
western, Pacific side. At
that time Spanish explorer
Gil González Dávila led an
expedition to indigenous
western settlements, where
he was greeted warmly and
given gifts of gold by local
chieftains. One of these
friendly chieftains was Chief
Nicarao, for whom Nicaragua was later named.
When González Dávila
moved farther inland, however, he had to fight off resistance from other local
tribes. A short time later,
another Spanish expedition
was successful in founding
two Spanish settlements in
western Nicaragua. One, at
León, near Lake Managua,
was founded in 1523, and
another, at Granada, near
Lake Nicaragua, was established in 1524. These two
settlements became the
centers of Spanish colonial
Nicaragua for the next three
centuries.

Soon after the Spanish
settlers arrived, the local
indigenous populations,

whom the Spanish called "Indians," were put to work as unpaid slaves, building settlements, growing crops, and searching for gold. The Spanish also made money by trading local Indians as part of the slave trade; indeed, an estimated 200,000 native Nicaraguans were exported to Spain's South American colonies between 1528 and 1540. An additional 300,000 to 400,000 local people died from diseases brought by the Spaniards or fled from Nicaragua. As Close explains,

Granada's Church of La Merced is a fine example of Spanish colonial architecture. The influence of the Catholic Church was particularly strong in Granada.

"In all . . . the native population declined from over one million to around ten thousand in the first six decades of Spanish rule."[4] Once the Indian population was depleted, Nicaragua suffered from a lack of laborers and never developed a prosperous economy as some other Spanish provinces did.

Another legacy of Spanish rule was a rivalry that developed between the two cities of León and Granada. Each became a commercial center servicing its surrounding agricultural areas, but the two cities developed very different cultures. Granada was settled by wealthy upper-class Spaniards and developed an economy based on cattle and trade. The people in Granada also established a close relationship with the Catholic Church and became known for their conservative, religious values. León, on the other hand, was settled largely by Spanish soldiers and became home to poor or middle-class artisans and merchants whose values were much more liberal. León ultimately became the political capital during Spanish rule, a development that caused great resentment

THE BRITISH INFLUENCE ON THE MOSQUITO COAST

As early as 1633, British explorers landed on the Mosquito Coast with plans to harvest timber and grow sugarcane. The British developed friendly relations with the Miskito Indian tribe, and together, the British and the Miskito dominated the Caribbean side of Nicaragua and resisted Spanish control over the area for many decades. In fact, British buccaneers became bold enough to make numerous raids during this period against Spanish settlements in the west. In 1665, for example, the British traveled as far as Lake Nicaragua, where they pillaged the important Spanish town of Granada. This British domination of the east was made official in 1740, when the Mosquito Coast was formally placed under the protection of the British government. Raids by British pirates stopped with a treaty signed by Britain, Spain, and France in 1783, but Britain continued to be interested in Nicaragua because of the possibility of building a canal that would link the Caribbean with the Pacific Ocean. Britain did not leave Nicaragua for good until the mid-1800s, when the United States began to take an active role in the region.

among the people of Granada, who had to submit to rule by what they considered to be a culturally inferior city.

Meanwhile, during the Spanish colonial rule of western Nicaragua, the British were making inroads in the eastern part of the region. British settlers and pirates, called buccaneers, befriended the Miskito Indians living on the Caribbean coast, conducted some trading activities, and carried out raids against Spanish ships traveling down the Río San Juan and against Spanish settlements in the east. This British influence on the Caribbean coast created a lasting legacy. As Close explains, it had the effect of "creat[ing] among the Miskitos a mistrust toward the Spaniards and their successors which underlies today's . . . conflict [between the Nicaraguan government and the Miskito]."[5]

Later in the eighteenth century, eastern Nicaragua became home to yet another people, Black Caribs, people of mixed black and Indian ancestry from the Carib tribe of the British West Indies. The British ousted them from the West Indies and they traveled to various areas in Central America, including the Mosquito Coast. By the end of the eighteenth century, Nicaragua's population totaled about 180,000 and was made up largely of mestizo people (of mixed Spanish and Indian blood) who lived in the Pacific region and a much smaller population on the Caribbean side of the country composed of three Indian tribes (the Miskito, Rama, and Sumu tribes) and Black Caribs.

INDEPENDENCE AND CIVIL WAR

The Spanish provinces in Central America declared their independence from Spain in 1821. The drive toward liberty in Nicaragua began as early as 1811, when León declared its independence, rapidly followed by Granada and other towns. As historians Nathan A. Haverstock and John P. Hoover explain, "Some Nicaraguans were deeply impressed by the success of both the French and the American Revolutions, and cherished the thought of becoming independent themselves."[6] These early Nicaraguan rebellions were put down by Spain with force, but following the creation of an independent empire in Mexico, all of Central America followed suit to announce their independence in 1821. Once independent, however, provinces had to decide whether to join Mexico's new empire or try to forge ahead alone.

Ultimately, in 1823, Nicaragua and four other Central American countries (Guatemala, El Salvador, Honduras, and Costa Rica) decided not to join Mexico and instead formed a federation called the United Provinces of Central America. The federation sought to establish democratic governments in each member nation under a loose federation rule. In Nicaragua, the establishment of the federation led only to civil war, as liberals in León fought with conservatives from Granada for control. The federation ultimately failed, and on April 30, 1838, Nicaragua declared its independence from the group.

Independence for Nicaragua, however, brought continuing violence and political strife that destroyed lives and property. The political unrest also prevented Nicaragua from developing a stable economy, despite the availability of a lucrative new agricultural product, coffee, that was enriching nearby nations.

AMERICAN INTERVENTION

Amid this turmoil and with Spain no longer in control, Nicaragua quickly became the pawn of British and American interests. The British had long had a presence on the Mosquito Coast and in 1848 moved to strengthen their control by seizing the port of San Juan del Norte at the mouth of the Río San Juan. This alarmed the United States, which had become interested in Nicaragua as a possible site for a canal linking the Caribbean Sea with the Pacific Ocean. American businessman Cornelius Vanderbilt led this effort and negotiated a contract with the country in 1849 that gave his company exclusive rights to build the canal. Nicaragua, for its part, encouraged the canal idea as an answer to its prayers for economic prosperity.

The United States and Britain ultimately agreed in the Clayton-Bulwer Treaty of 1850 that neither should claim exclusive control in Nicaragua, but their involvement set the stage for years of foreign intervention in Nicaragua's affairs. As Walker explains, "Both countries frequently took sides in Nicaraguan domestic politics—the British tending to support the Conservatives, and the Americans [tending] to support the Liberals."[7] This foreign intervention only exacerbated the already contentious political divisions in Nicaragua.

Toward the end of the nineteenth century, U.S. interest in Nicaragua waned temporarily as the building of a railroad in

THE WILLIAM WALKER INVASION

One of the most destructive episodes of American meddling in Nicaragua occurred in 1855 when an American soldier of fortune, William Walker, seized control of the government of Nicaragua. Walker and his small army were supported both by Liberals in Nicaragua and by private businessmen in the United States who wanted to reestablish slavery in Nicaragua. Notably, the U.S. government did not object to Walker's activities, even though the British and neighboring Central American countries raised strong objections to Walker's bold move. Walker was driven out of the country two years later, after the governments of four other Central American nations sent troops to Nicaragua. The British encouraged and funded the war against Walker as a way to limit U.S. influence in the country. For Nicaraguans, however, the war was even more costly; thousands lost their lives, and the city of Granada was burned.

Panama took precedence over the proposed Nicaraguan canal. Later, however, the United States again intervened strongly in Nicaraguan affairs. In 1909, for example, the U.S. government sent four hundred marines to the country in support of a political coup that successfully overthrew Liberal dictator José Santos Zelaya, whose policies had antagonized the United States. The marines returned in 1912 to maintain order during another political crisis and remained in Nicaragua almost continually until 1933. During this period, the United States also closely supervised Nicaragua's financial and economic policies and controlled the country's political system. Another example of U.S. control over Nicaragua was the Chamorro-Bryan Treaty of 1916, a treaty that generously gave the United States the exclusive option, in perpetuity, to develop a canal in Nicaragua, a renewable lease on the Corn Islands in the Caribbean, and the right to build a naval base on the Pacific coast. As Close describes, "By World War I Nicaragua had become as much an American protectorate as the Mosquito Coast had been a British one."[8]

SANDINO AND AMERICAN WITHDRAWAL

American control over Nicaragua ended largely due to the efforts of a Nicaraguan rebel named Augusto César Sandino.

AUGUSTO SANDINO, NICARAGUAN HERO

Augusto Sandino is one of Nicaragua's most honored heroes. He was born the illegitimate son of a peasant woman and her married boss in the small town of Niquinohomo, near Managua. His mother abandoned him and he was raised by his father, who never completely accepted him. Despite this troubled beginning, Sandino grew up to become an eloquent speaker and writer with a passion for his country. He strongly opposed U.S. intervention in Nicaragua's affairs and saw the United States as the enemy of Nicaragua. In the 1920s, Sandino, using some of his personal funds, bought weapons and convinced some peasants to help him stage attacks on U.S. businesses in Nicaragua. Over time, Sandino developed a hit-and-run

run style of fighting that became known as guerrilla warfare, and his patriotic message inspired many to follow him. By 1931 Sandino and his troops were able to occupy most of central, northern, and eastern Nicaragua. Sandino is credited with forcing U.S. marines to leave the country. However, Sandino's attacks also led to the creation of a Nicaraguan military force called the National Guard, which later assassinated Sandino and helped Anastasio Somoza become one of Nicaragua's most brutal dictators.

Augusto Sandino is celebrated for forcing U.S. troops out of Nicaragua in the late 1920s.

Outraged by the U.S. occupation and domination of his country, Sandino began a war to remove the Americans from Nicaragua in 1927. By developing guerrilla war techniques such as harassment and hit-and-run attacks, and with support from poor peasants, Sandino's forces effectively bogged the American troops down in a costly war that they could never completely win.

In response to Sandino's attacks, U.S. soldiers used tactics such as air raids. These only increased the local support for

Sandino. The United States also formed a Nicaraguan military force called the National Guard to fight the Sandino forces. The United States approved a young Liberal, General Anastasio Somoza García, to head the National Guard.

Finally, after negotiations, Sandino agreed to stop fighting if American forces withdrew from Nicaragua. The U.S. marines were withdrawn in 1933, and Sandino, true to his word, laid down his arms and made plans to set up peaceful agricultural cooperatives in the mountains. However, the following year (1934) Sandino was murdered on Somoza's orders by National Guardsmen after he attended a presidential dinner in Managua. This occurred without the approval or knowledge of the duly elected Nicaraguan president, Juan Bautista Sacasa. The National Guard, since the American withdrawal, had become a force unto itself, led by the ambitious Somoza.

THE SOMOZA DYNASTY

After eliminating Sandino and his followers, Somoza soon gained control of Nicaragua, and began a dynasty through which he, his family, and friends ruled the country as repressive military dictators for forty-three years. Somoza first maneuvered to force the resignation of President Sacasa in 1936 and then installed one of his supporters as president. On January 1, 1937, Somoza finally assumed the office of president himself. In this position, he rewrote the constitution to allow himself to stay in power and set up a government system that gave him complete control over Nicaragua. To do this, he strengthened the power and reach of the National Guard and used it to intimidate and murder anyone who dared oppose his will. At the same time, he rewarded his supporters with generous bribes to retain their loyalty.

In addition, Somoza did everything in his power to establish good relations with the United States, an international ally he believed was essential to keeping him in power. He tried to maintain the illusion of a democratic government by holding sham elections, setting up two essentially powerless political parties, and pretending that the Nicaraguan parliament and constitution were not under his control. In 1947 Somoza even stepped down from the presidency to appease U.S. political demands. Thereafter, he installed supporters or family members into the presidential position and exercised his power just as effectively from the sidelines. Nicaragua also backed U.S. foreign policies and volunteered political, logistical, and military support for American interventions around the world. During World War II, for example, Somoza permitted the United States to build naval and air bases in Nicaragua. Because of these gestures, the U.S. government formed an uneasy alliance with Somoza's government.

Somoza used his great power to enrich himself, his family, and his friends at the expense of the Nicaraguan poor. Funds that could have been used for schools, health care, and roads instead went into Somoza's pockets, and the vast majority of Nicaraguans remained impoverished and illiterate. These actions ultimately led to the creation of a secret opposition movement that plotted to kill Somoza. On September 21, 1956, Rigoberto López Pérez, a young

Anastasio Somoza (left) rides in an automobile with U.S. president Franklin Roosevelt during a 1939 visit. Somoza and his sons ruled Nicaragua as dictators.

Nicaraguan poet, shot Somoza at point-blank range. Despite efforts by surgeons to save him, Somoza died several days later on September 28.

Somoza's death, however, did not end his regime. His sons, Luís and Anastasio, took up the reins of power and ruled Nicaragua for many more decades. Luís, the elder son, became president, and Anastasio became the head of the National Guard. In 1963 Luís turned the presidency over to trusted friends. In 1967, when Luís was in poor health, his brother Anastasio became president. Luís died two months later. During their rule, the two brothers successfully defeated a number of rebel revolts and continued their father's legacy of corruption and repression. They also succeeded in retaining U.S. support, despite their antidemocratic policies.

THE SANDINISTA REVOLUTION

In 1979 the Somoza dynasty finally came to an end due to the efforts of the FSLN (Frente Sandinista de Liberación Nacional, or Sandinista National Liberation Front), an opposition guerrilla group that developed mass popular support for its fight against the Somoza regime. The FSLN, also known as the Sandinistas, was founded as early as 1961, but its early strikes against Somoza forces were quickly defeated by the government. The tide turned against the Somozas on December 23, 1972, when a massive earthquake struck Managua, killing an estimated thirty thousand people and leaving much of the city homeless. Instead of restoring order and using foreign aid to provide relief to Nicaraguans, Anastasio Somoza permitted National Guard members to loot stores and businesses and diverted foreign relief monies to further enrich himself and his supporters. According to Close, "Only $16 million of the $32 million sent by the American government was acknowledged as received by Nicaraguan authorities."[9] Somoza's response to the suffering and disorder created by the earthquake destroyed almost all remaining support for the government and provided a chance for the opposition to make its move against the regime.

Following the earthquake disaster, the FSLN became increasingly successful and well known in Nicaragua. A 1974 raid by the FSLN against Somoza's minister of agriculture

Sandinista guerrillas ride on a Managuan bus they hijacked in 1978. That year the Sandinistas raided the legislature and took fifteen hundred hostages.

was particularly effective at enhancing the image of the rebel group. In that raid, FSLN guerrillas captured a number of Somoza supporters and relatives as hostages, and extracted a high ransom and other concessions from the Somoza government. Later, Somoza made the FSLN pay for its success by increasing the National Guard's attacks against the group. By 1976, many FSLN guerrillas had been killed, taken prisoner, or forced to hide. The government crackdown, however, had the effect of increasing international human rights criticism of the Somoza regime and alienating the U.S. Congress against Nicaragua. At the same time, the difficulties faced by the FSLN split the group into three different factions, which weakened the opposition's power and prevented the FSLN from taking advantage of international scrutiny of Somoza's tactics.

The pressure on the Somoza government continued when even the conservative forces in Nicaragua began calling for an end to the country's dictatorship. In response, in 1978 Somoza's forces assassinated Pedro Joaquín Chamorro, the publisher of *La Prensa*, one of the country's largest conservative newspapers. The incident brought more than fifty thousand Nicaraguans to the street, where they protested and called for Somoza to step down. The FSLN capitalized on this civil unrest by staging "Operation Pigsty," a daring raid on the Nicaraguan legislature that took fifteen hundred hostages, including many of Somoza's relatives. This raid was followed by a nationwide business strike and a wave of popular unrest. Anastasio Somoza sent out his National Guard to put down the rebellion and vowed to stay in office. Ultimately, however, the United States concluded that Somoza would have to go and initiated negotiations to try to resolve the conflict. Sensing an opportunity, the FSLN launched an offensive in June 1979 that succeeded in gaining the support of many cities in Nicaragua.

Somoza finally resigned on July 17, 1979, handing over power to the FSLN. As guidebook writer Hazel Plunkett describes, "On July 19, 1979, television footage was broadcast around the world depicting the victorious Sandinista troops marching triumphantly into Managua."[10] Once in power, the Sandinistas pledged to work for greater political freedoms, a better economy, and a foreign policy more independent of the United States. This change marked a turning point for Nicaragua, and inspired among most Nicaraguans hope for democracy and the promise of a better future.

3

Democracy in Nicaragua

Nicaragua's struggles continued even after its dictators were overthrown and a democratic government system was put in place. Soon after the Sandinista revolution, the United States, Nicaragua's main trading partner, halted aid and trade to the country and supported military efforts to overthrow the new government. This foreign intervention, combined with natural disasters and other events, contributed to more political instability in Nicaragua and to prolonged economic difficulties that continue to test the Nicaraguan people even today.

Sandinista Rule

In 1979 the Sandinistas inherited a country in ruins from years of political turmoil. The economy was depressed; the country owed $1.5 billion in debts to the United States; and many Nicaraguans were living as refugees in other countries, leaving the remaining population barely surviving amid widespread poverty and disease. The new government, therefore, sought to stabilize Nicaragua politically while taking steps to help the poor, restructure the economy, secure foreign aid, and improve human rights. Most Nicaraguans supported these efforts and considered the Sandinistas their best chance of recovering from the Somoza years. According to Walker, "The mood in the country in July 1979 was one of near universal ecstasy."[11]

At the forefront of the Sandinista agenda was a desire to improve the lives of ordinary Nicaraguans. As social scientist Dennis Gilbert put it, "The new leadership was conscious of the social inequities produced during the previous thirty years of unrestricted economic growth and was determined to make the country's workers and peasants . . . the prime beneficiaries of the new society."[12] One of the first programs implemented by the government was a national literacy crusade launched in 1980 to teach all Nicaraguans to read and write. The program was affordable because the Sandinistas were able to mobilize large numbers of volunteers who traveled throughout the countryside. Health education was also vital; health campaigns provided vaccinations and taught people about the causes of disease and the need to clean wells, build latrines, and eliminate mosquito breeding grounds. To provide jobs, the government initiated a variety of public works projects financed from a special fund to combat unemployment. The Sandinistas also focused on providing food and rebuilding agriculture, which had been decimated by the war against Somoza. To do this, the government provided aid and technical assistance both to poor peasant farmers and to wealthier farm families.

The cornerstone of the early Sandinista social programs, however, was a series of land reforms put in place by the Agrarian Reform Law. By the end of the Somoza rule, the Somoza family owned at least one-fifth of all agricultural land

Crowds of Nicaraguans cheer as victorious Sandinistas ride atop a tank in Managua's main square in 1979.

and one-fourth of all industrial wealth. In the land reforms, the government seized these assets and redistributed them to state farms and collectives that were to be run by the poor. Later, as a result of peasants' resistance to collectives, the government began to give land directly to individual poor farmers.

The Sandinistas also made strides in other areas. They reorganized the armed forces and equipped them with modern weapons, purchased largely from the Soviet Union. To maintain the country's international credit standing, the new government agreed to pay off Somoza's debt to foreign countries and negotiated with the international banking community for acceptable terms. Human rights were largely respected by the Sandinistas: Somoza supporters were investigated and tried; the death penalty was abolished; and newspapers such as *La Prensa*, which harshly criticized the Sandinistas, were granted freedom of the press. The government also sought to build a broad-based economy. It provided financial assistance to maintain Nicaragua's private-sector businesses and brought many wealthy conservatives into the Sandinista government.

WOMEN GUERRILLA FIGHTERS

Women played an important role in the Sandinista revolution in Nicaragua. They worked in undercover operations and as guerrilla fighters, and some even became leaders in the Sandinista National Liberation Front. After the Sandinistas came to power, a number of women served in Nicaragua's government. One of the most well-known female guerrilla leaders in Nicaragua was Doris Tijerino. She joined the FSLN in the 1960s and is best remembered for taking part in defending the home of an important FSLN member that was attacked by Somoza forces in 1969. Tijerino was captured during the fight, imprisoned, and tortured by the National Guard. Another important female FSLN member was Dora María Tellez, who helped the Sandinistas capture government hostages during a 1978 raid on the National Palace. The raid forced Somoza to release FSLN prisoners, including Tijerino. Tijerino later became head of police and Tellez became the minister of health in the new Sandinista government.

NICARAGUA'S CONSTITUTION AND DEMOCRATIC GOVERNMENT

Yet another achievement of the Sandinistas was the creation of a new democratic framework for Nicaragua's government. In 1987 a new constitution was adopted that established a democratic system of government based on a separation of powers and a guarantee of civil liberties. The constitution also provided for a strong presidency, a one-house legislature, and an independent judiciary. All citizens over the age of sixteen were permitted to vote. This constitution, with certain reforms made in 1995 and 2000, still governs Nicaragua today.

Under the Sandinista constitution, as reformed, the president of Nicaragua is given broad powers. The president is assisted by a vice president and performs typical executive tasks, such as acting as commander in chief of the military, appointing a cabinet, and proposing a budget. In addition, the Nicaraguan president is given certain extraordinary powers, such as the right to suspend constitutional rights during national emergencies. The constitution mandates a five-year term. Neither the president nor a close relative is allowed to be reelected for a second, consecutive term.

The one-house Nicaraguan legislature, called the National Assembly, also has significant powers that were expanded under the 1995 reforms. Its ninety-two members, like the president, are elected for five-year terms. The assembly proposes and enacts legislation, can override a presidential veto by a simple majority, and must approve the presidential budget. The National Assembly also approves members of the Supreme Court nominated by the president, ratifies treaties, and approves or rejects presidential declarations of national emergencies.

The judicial branch of government, under the Nicaraguan constitution, consists of an independent Supreme Court made up of sixteen justices. The justices are appointed for five-year terms and can only be removed for certain lawful reasons. The Supreme Court has the power to determine the constitutionality of laws and to resolve disputes between the executive and legislative branches. In addition, the court appoints judges to the country's lower courts, called the courts of the first instance, which are located in major cities.

The constitution also creates an independent fourth branch of government called the Supreme Electoral Council.

In 2005 President Enrique Bolaños (at podium, right) addresses the National Assembly, Nicaragua's legislative body.

The council is made up of seven magistrates who organize and regulate elections in Nicaragua. The magistrates are elected to five-year terms by the National Assembly.

In 1990 a system of local government was created by the Sandinista National Assembly. This system includes a municipal council for each of more than a hundred municipal units. Citizens vote for representatives to serve on this council, and the council members then select a leader, or mayor. The local councils control urban development, land use, sanitation, environmental protection, road maintenance, public construction, property taxes, and similar matters.

THE CONTRA WAR AND PEACE ACCORDS

Throughout the first couple of years of Sandinista rule, the United States, under the leadership of President Jimmy Carter, cautiously accepted the new Nicaraguan government and provided some economic aid to the impoverished country. In 1981, however, the newly elected Ronald Reagan administration in the United States began a campaign to undermine the Sandinista government. Reagan was an ardent anti-Communist, and the Sandinista government was developing military relationships with Communist governments, such as Cuba and the Soviet Union. U.S. officials also worried that Nicaragua was supporting rebels in El Salvador's civil war. Reacting to these concerns, Reagan suspended all U.S. aid to the country on January 23, 1981. He also provided financial and other support to a rebel group called the Contras, who began a hit-and-run guerrilla war against the Sandinista government from bases in neighboring countries such as Honduras and Costa Rica.

The loss of U.S. aid and the Contra war caused serious damage to the already weak Nicaraguan economy. Instead of continuing social and agricultural programs, the Sandinista government was forced to spend precious national funds on the military. As a result, most social programs suffered and agricultural production declined sharply. As Walker explains, "In the second half of the [1980s] the war-related expenditures . . . consumed over half of the national budget, thus inevitably depriving social programs of badly needed resources."[13] As the war escalated, the government also declared a state of national emergency and temporarily suspended certain political and press freedoms. Suspects believed to be associated with the Contras were detained, and newspapers such as *La Prensa* were heavily censored. These new policies, in turn, slowly undermined popular support for the Sandinista government. The Catholic Church, once supportive of the Sandinistas, became critical of the government, and peasants became impatient with the government's slowing reform efforts.

Nevertheless, the government went forward with its plans to organize the country's first set of democratic elections. On November 4, 1984, elections were held and deemed by most foreign observers to be fair and free.

Protestors demonstrating against U.S. aid to Nicaragua's Contra rebels at a 1986 rally included this man wearing a mask of U.S. president Ronald Reagan.

Approximately 75 percent of Nicaraguans went to the polls. The FSLN won 67 percent of the vote, electing Sandinista leader Daniel Ortega as Nicaragua's president and giving the FSLN a majority of seats in the new National Assembly.

Soon after his election, however, Ortega faced escalating pressure from the United States. In April 1985, after the U.S. Congress halted continued funding of the Contras, the Reagan administration ordered a total embargo on Nicaragua's trade with the United States, formerly Nicaragua's largest trading partner. Later, U.S. aid to the Contras was reinstated in the amount of $100 million, adding more pressure on the Sandinista government. These developments forced the government to devote even more resources to

DANIEL ORTEGA, SANDINISTA LEADER

Daniel Ortega, head of the Sandinista National Liberation Front, led Nicaragua in the 1979 revolution that overthrew the brutal Somoza dictatorship. He was born in 1946 to poor parents who strongly opposed the dictatorship. His hero as a young man was Augusto Sandino, a rebel who had forced U.S. troops out of Nicaragua in 1933. In 1963 Ortega joined the FSLN and later became its leader. His efforts to overthrow Somoza won the support of both peasants and intellectuals, and by the time the Sandinistas took power, Ortega had become a national hero.

Ortega continued to lead the FSLN as head of the Sandinista government, and his popularity continued as a result of policies that provided the poor with access to land, education, and health care for the first time in their lives. He became the country's first democratically elected president in 1984. Both Ortega and the FSLN, however, lost favor with Nicaraguans during the Contra war, because of cutbacks in government programs, divisions within the FSLN, and accusations of corruption. The FSLN lost in the next three presidential elections, but Ortega is expected to run again in the 2006 elections.

President Ortega (right) hands out land deeds to Nicaraguan peasants in 1985.

military defense and away from economic and social development.

Finally, in 1986, the pressure on the Sandinista government eased when the Contras were severely weakened by a political scandal in America. The Iran-Contra scandal erupted when it was discovered that Reagan administration officials had made efforts to secretly continue aid to the Contras during the 1985 congressional ban. As a result of the scandal, the U.S. Congress once again cut off military aid to the Contras in 1987. The resulting pause in fighting made conditions ripe for negotiations. Oscar Arias Sánchez, the newly elected president of neighboring Costa Rica, quickly took advantage of the situation to negotiate a regional plan to bring peace not only to Nicaragua but to other countries in Central America that were experiencing similar civil conflicts. In Nicaragua, the Arias peace plan led in 1988 to a cease-fire and amnesty agreement between the government and the Contras, to the reinstatement of political and press freedoms, and to the scheduling of new democratic elections for February 1990.

The Arias plan brought a shaky peace to Nicaragua, but by this time, the country's economy was shattered. The loss of U.S. aid, the devastating trade embargo, and the many years of war had completely bankrupted the country. Inflation had skyrocketed. Making matters worse, in October 1988 Nicaragua was hit by Hurricane Joan, which killed 432 people, left 180,000 homeless, and caused $1 billion in property damage. The hurricane was followed by a severe drought in 1989 that wiped out most of that year's agricultural harvest.

THE CHAMORRO PRESIDENCY (1990–1996)

The 1990 elections took place as a result of the Arias peace plan, according to the new constitution enacted by the Sandinistas in 1987, and amid continuing tensions between the Contras and the government. International attention was also intense; United Nations observers were deployed to closely observe the election and make sure it was fair. The Sandinistas were confident they would be reelected. However, a new opposition coalition—the UNO (Unión Nacional Opositora, or National Opposition Union)—led by conservative Violeta Chamorro and backed by the United States, won a surprise victory over the FSLN.

In 1988 the town of Bluefields on Nicaragua's Atlantic coast lies in ruins after Hurricane Joan pummeled the country.

The stunning election results have been explained by observers as an expression of Nicaraguans' strong desire for peace: Many people feared that reelecting the FSLN would only continue the Contra conflict. In addition, Nicaraguans desperately wanted prosperity. By this point, as Walker points out, "Nicaragua had dropped to the unenviable status of being the poorest country in the western hemisphere."[14] Chamorro won by promising to improve the private-sector economy and to reconcile the political divisions within the country. Despite the shock of its loss, the FSLN accepted the defeat and handed over power with a graceful concession speech and congratulations for the new president. As Plunkett notes, "[Chamorro's] election marked the first peaceful transfer of power from government to opposition in Nicaragua's history."[15]

Chamorro owed her victory, in large part, to the United States. The United States had funded and organized the UNO coalition and had encouraged the Contras to keep up the pressure on the Sandinistas during the election even though their raids violated the Arias peace accords. After her election, the United States finally called off its trade and aid embargoes against Nicaragua.

CONTINUING ECONOMIC AND POLITICAL PROBLEMS

Despite this U.S. support, however, Chamorro faced daunting challenges when she took office in April 1990. First, she was not a seasoned politician but, rather, the relatively uneducated and inexperienced wife of Pedro Joaquín Chamorro, the publisher of the conservative newspaper *La Prensa* who had been murdered by Somoza's followers years earlier. Her coalition was weak and sharply divided, and it immediately began to unravel.

In addition, Chamorro had to cope with the still powerful Sandinistas, who controlled the armed forces and many other parts of government and had a strong base of support among the Nicaraguan population. Chamorro opted to negotiate and share power with the FSLN, a strategy that was heavily criticized by many within her own government. The agreement with the Sandinistas allowed them to retain control over the army and promised not to reverse Sandinista land reforms. These concessions, however, were not enough for many who supported the Sandinistas; some peasants and others wanted to see the Sandinistas take a stronger stand against Chamorro's policies. The result was that Nicaragua continued to be a very divided nation.

THE ARIAS PEACE PLAN

The U.S.-funded Contra war against the Sandinista government in Nicaragua ended largely due to the efforts of Oscar Arias Sánchez, the president of Costa Rica, Nicaragua's southern neighbor. In 1986, when Arias was elected, much of Central America was in conflict. In addition to Contra attacks on the Sandinista government, there were rebels fighting the governments in both El Salvador and Guatemala, and various border disputes between several other countries.

In order to ease this situation, the presidents of Colombia, Mexico, Panama, and Venezuela (known as the Contadora Group) met in 1984 to discuss ways to solve the conflicts. The peace effort, however, did not become a reality until 1987, when President Arias took the lead to propose a regional peace plan. The plan called for withdrawal of foreign advisers, cease-fires, and democratic elections in five Central American countries—Nicaragua, El Salvador, Guatemala, Costa Rica, and Honduras. The plan was signed by all five countries on August 7, 1987, and is credited with bringing peace to the region. Arias was awarded the Nobel Peace Prize in 1987 for his efforts.

Amid this political chaos, Chamorro now also had the full responsibility of improving the devastated Nicaraguan economy, which was marked by rampant poverty and unemployment, low production, destroyed roads and infrastructure, and high foreign debt. These economic issues were made all the worse when the United States, along with international financial institutions, made foreign aid and loans dependent on Nicaragua's immediately promoting a private economy and imposing economic austerity measures aimed at halting inflation, reducing government spending, and increasing exports. Two well-known international groups, the International Monetary Fund (IMF) and the World Bank, for example, demanded that Nicaragua take difficult steps such as cutting the public workforce; reducing spending for health, education, and other social programs; and changing its economy from one based on agriculture to one that would attract foreign investment.

In exchange for $300 million in U.S. aid, Chamorro implemented many of the U.S. and international economic demands. These included cuts in spending, the firing of many public employees, and a 50 percent cut in the army. Chamorro also pushed for privatization of collectives and companies owned by the government. These policies, however, ultimately violated the government's promises to retain the Sandinista land

In 1995 President Violeta Chamorro visits children displaced by the eruption of Cerro Negro, a volcano near the village of Malpaisillo.

reforms, created great hardships for the Nicaraguan people, and led to public strikes against the Chamorro government. Public protests in 1990, 1993, and 1994, for example, crippled the country and created a state of dangerous civil unrest.

Moreover, although the Contras were supposed to have disbanded and disarmed, they found favor with many in the Chamorro government, which was reluctant to subdue them by force. Contras often appeared with weapons at the strikes or conducted raids in outlying areas in the countryside, raising the threat of a continuing civil war. The Chamorro presidency was also plagued in 1992 by more natural disasters, including a drought that destroyed important export crops and a tidal wave that left thousands of Nicaraguans homeless.

In the end, Chamorro made little progress in solving the core problems facing Nicaraguans. Although she established a free-market economy, the country remained deeply in debt and unable to support itself. In addition, at the end of her presidency, political divisions remained sharp, and most Nicaraguans were unemployed and poorer than ever before.

RECENT ELECTIONS

In the next elections, held in 1996, the Sandinistas lost again, this time to a Liberal candidate, Arnoldo Alemán, who had the support of wealthy Nicaraguans. Alemán grew up in a farming family that supported the Somoza dictatorship, and much of his family's property was confiscated by the Sandinista government. Alemán strongly opposed the Sandinistas and became mayor of Managua in 1990, during the Chamorro presidency. As mayor, he built a number of shopping malls, gas stations, and fast food outlets, accomplishments that he touted as signs of vigorous economic progress. During his campaign for the presidency, Alemán promised to fight poverty and unemployment by encouraging these types of modernization and large-scale foreign investment. He impressed many as a strong and forceful leader who might deliver what Chamorro could not: economic recovery and prosperity.

Once Alemán was elected, however, his ambitious promises were not carried out. Although he tried to create stable conditions for more foreign investment, stability continued to elude Nicaragua as armed bands of Contras and others roamed the countryside. In 1998 Alemán renewed agreements with the IMF and World Bank largely under the same conditions imposed on Chamorro. These included tough austerity programs that pushed even more people into poverty and unemployment and cut social spending at the same time. Disputes also continued concerning land confiscated during Sandinista land reforms. Alemán's supporters pressured him to reverse the reforms and return the properties to their wealthy owners, while peasants and small farmers fought to keep their lands. In addition, Alemán's administration, like others before him, was set back by another devastating hurricane (Hurricane Mitch) in 1998. The massive storm destroyed more than $1 billion of property, left at least 800,000 homeless, and killed between 3,000 and 8,000 people. Finally, toward the end of his term, allegations of corruption arose within Alemán's government. After leaving office, Alemán himself was accused of having stolen more than $100 million in government funds. He was later tried, convicted, and sentenced to twenty years in prison on these charges.

Despite their mounting frustration with their leaders, Nicaraguans turned out in large numbers in the next set of elections. In 2001 they elected Enrique Bolaños Geyer, an affable, older businessman who was Alemán's vice president and whose campaign focused largely on rooting out government corruption. After taking office, Bolaños unleashed a remarkable crusade against corruption in Nicaraguan politics. He proposed new anticorruption laws, reduced the bloated salaries of top government officials, and helped bring Alemán to justice. Bolaños also made headway on the economic front. He was able to secure a major loan from the IMF plus partial debt forgiveness from some of Nicaragua's creditors. In fact, Bolaños earned a reputation around the world for honesty, strong leadership, and upholding democracy. As political analyst Claudia Paguaga explains, "The election of Enrique Bolaños in Nicaragua was above all a victory for democracy."[16]

Despite these successes, Bolaños lost support within Nicaragua. Many liberal members of the National Assembly remained loyal to Alemán in spite of his illegal acts, and most

Saluting the crowd, former president Arnoldo Alemán is escorted to prison in 2004 for embezzling government funds.

turned against Bolaños because of his pursuit of Alemán. In addition, the Sandinistas joined the liberals in opposing Bolaños.

Despite some economic advances and new ethical leadership, Nicaragua still faces an uncertain future filled with the continuing and familiar problems of economic recovery, social unrest, and political instability.

4

THE PEOPLE OF NICARAGUA

Embattled by years of political struggles and instability, and divided by their history into two different societies, Nicaraguans have yet to escape the grip of poverty and widespread unemployment. Yet they have remained dedicated to their traditions and values, and are anxious to improve themselves and their country.

NICA VERSUS *COSTEÑO* SOCIETY

Nicaragua's population of about 5.3 million people is made up mostly of mestizos, people of mixed Spanish and Indian ancestry, and whites. Indeed, mestizos make up about 69 percent of the total population, and those classified as whites make up another 17 percent, combining to form an 86 percent majority. No clear line separates whites from mestizos, but those with lighter skin tones appear to have more social and economic advantages. People in this majority speak Spanish, call themselves Nicas, and share a Latino/Hispanic heritage and culture. Most of this majority population lives on the Pacific coastal plains, and many live in urban areas such as Managua and surrounding suburbs. These western-dwelling Nicaraguans have a strong national identity and tend to be interested and involved in elections and national affairs.

The Caribbean side of Nicaragua, on the other hand, is home to Nicaragua's small minority ethnic populations, who collectively call themselves *costeños*. Isolated from the west by rugged mountains and rain forests, this eastern part of the country was never part of the Spanish empire and was instead affiliated much more with the British. These factors caused Caribbean Nicaragua to become divided by both history and culture from the western side of the country. In fact, as Gilbert puts it, "In many ways, [the eastern, or Caribbean, hinterland] is a completely different country from the Spanish-speaking nation to the west."[17]

Costeño minority groups include three Indian tribes: the Miskito, Sumu, and Rama. In addition, the Caribbean area is inhabited by a community of blacks made up of Creoles, descendants of Europeans and black Africans brought to Nicaragua as slaves, and Garifuna, Black Caribs who have a mixed West Indian and African ancestry. In recent years, these ethnic groups have been joined by a growing population of mestizos who have moved from the west to find new opportunities. Most *costeños* speak English instead of Spanish, and many also speak an indigenous language. Most are Protestant rather than Catholic.

Children of Hispanic descent pose before a mural in Cuidad Sandino, near Managua.

The Miskito, Nicaragua's largest ethnic group, are concentrated in the northeastern part of this territory, near the border with Honduras, which also has a sizable Miskito population. The Miskito have a long cultural history of living together and sharing land and resources communally, that is, without individual ownership. This tradition has ended, but as Hazel Plunkett describes, "Their collective relationship with the rainforest and their emphasis on living in harmony with nature have still not broken down and are enduring features of Miskito culture."[18] Today, as with other indigenous groups, the Miskito are generally poor, uneducated, and either unemployed or working in low-wage jobs. Many, for example, work in dangerous underground jobs in Nicaraguan mines. A much smaller group of Sumu Indians can be found farther south, inland from Puerto Cabezas. The Rama, the smallest Indian group, are located largely on Rama Cay, an island near the southern town of Bluefields.

The Caribbean coast's black community lives mainly in the coastal cities of Bluefields and Puerto Cabezas. The lifestyle among this community is very different from that on the Pacific, Hispanic side of the country. It is much more relaxed and similar to typical Caribbean cultures. Yet of all the eastern ethnic groups, blacks are the most urban, educated,

MISKITO AUTONOMY

Miskito Indians living in the Caribbean region of Nicaragua have long distrusted the Spanish culture and government that developed in the Pacific side of the country. The Sandinista government sought to unite the two parts of the country, but its actions further alienated the Miskito. The Sandinistas, for example, relocated more than ten thousand Miskito Indian's from their homelands during the Contra war. In the 1980s, thousands of Miskito organized to fight for independence. Some even fought alongside Contras against the government. In response, the Sandinistas began negotiations with the Miskito, and an agreement was reached to provide limited autonomy to the Miskito in exchange for their disarmament. The agreement became law in 1987, and provided for two regional assemblies in the Caribbean with the power to govern local matters. In recent years, however, conflicts reappeared over logging of indigenous lands and other issues, leading the national government to halt funding to the east. The Miskito responded by setting up their own governing body in Puerto Cabezas, which

they call "Bilwi." Attitudes have clearly hardened, continuing the deep division between east and west in Nicaragua.

A family of Miskito Indians is transported to a relocation camp in 1985.

and skilled, and they rank at the top of the social and economic hierarchy in the east, second only to a few middle-class mestizos. Most eastern-dwelling mestizos, however, are poor and can be found in the interior parts of the lowlands, where they work in mining areas or carve out farms from the rain forests. Their presence in eastern Nicaragua has led to conflict with indigenous tribes, who are concerned about the loss of what they view as their ancient, communal lands.

Historically, the Miskito and other *costeños* do not regard themselves as Nicaraguans and have resisted what they regard as "Spanish rule" by the Nicaraguan government. During most of the Somoza period, the Caribbean side of the country was largely ignored by the government. The Sandinistas, however, tried to integrate the two parts of Nicaragua. After several actions by the government that angered the Miskito and caused many to take up arms to fight for independence from the rest of Nicaragua, the Sandinistas eventually negotiated with *costeño* representatives. The two sides agreed to insert provisions in the 1987 constitution to give the Caribbean coast region a degree of autonomy and self-rule while still remaining part of Nicaragua. Nevertheless, the relationship between the eastern region and the central government remains very tense, and many Miskito continue to favor full independence.

TRADITION AND FAMILY VALUES

For all Nicaraguans, and especially those that are part of the western Hispanic culture, family and traditional values are very important. In wealthier families, the definition of family is usually a patriarchal one in which the couple is formally married and the man is the head of the household. Among the poor, however, couples rarely marry before living together, and many families are run by women. Throughout the society families tend to be large, and extended families composed of several generations often live together in one house, share their belongings, and support each other in both family and business affairs. Even for those who move away from their family, social life often involves regular trips to stay in touch with family members.

For the wealthy, kinship includes family fortunes that are carefully guarded and passed from one generation to the

In 2004 family members help carry the belongings of a relative whose home was threatened by mud slides. Life in Nicaragua revolves around the family.

next. The emphasis on kinship also can be seen in the tendency for some Nicaraguans to add the surnames of their ancestors to their names in order to make clear their family history. Family connections, too, can often influence where people work. In the countryside, sons and daughters often farm small parcels of land that are part of or near land owned by their fathers, grandfathers, or other relatives. In the cities, people look to their relatives, even distant ones, for help in finding jobs or for other economic assistance. In times of crisis, this same pattern holds true, and relatives are expected to come to the aid of their kin.

The family relationship even extends beyond those who are related by blood or marriage. Through the practice of *compadrazgo*, parents choose an unrelated godfather (*padrino*) and godmother (*madrina*) to help support their child. Although this is also done in other countries, in Nicaragua the godparent relationship is taken much more seriously. Here, godparents are expected to take an active role in the child's life and to come to the aid of the child or the family during difficult times. Often, the godparents are close friends of the parents, but poorer families sometimes choose wealthy landowners, prosperous businessmen, or political leaders as godparents because they have the means to provide desperately needed economic help to their children.

THE CATHOLIC CHURCH AND OTHER RELIGIONS

Along with family values, Nicaraguans' religious affiliations have been an important part of most people's lives for many years. The Spanish established the Roman Catholic Church in Nicaragua in the sixteenth century and it quickly became the official faith in the region throughout colonial times. In 1939 the Nicaraguan constitution was changed to provide for a secular state and for freedom of religion, but the Catholic Church still continued to be very influential in Nicaragua. Church authorities were expected to take an active role in the nation's affairs, and their opinions on national issues were given great deference. In fact, during the Sandinista revolution, Catholic priests actively supported the FSLN and its dedication to social reform and helping the poor. Even today, the church plays a prominent role in the education system and in the country's social life. Most private schools are run by Catholic institutions, and across Nicaragua towns hold annual fiestas to celebrate various saints.

Nevertheless, the power of the Catholic Church has declined over the years. Today, most Catholic churches and priests are located in the cities, and even in these urban areas, many people no longer attend services regularly. Often, families visit the church mostly for formal ceremonies, such as those held for baptisms and funerals. Other remnants of Catholicism still evident in Nicaraguan culture, though, include a widespread belief in the power of saints, who are seen as the intermediaries between humans and God. Many families display pictures of saints in their homes and offer prayers to saints who are believed to have special powers. In addition, whole communities adopt a particular saint as their patron or helper.

The Sandinistas encouraged freedom of religion, and other religions have grown to rival the influence of the Catholic Church. Today, close to a third of Nicaraguans follow Protestant religions established by the British as well as many new evangelical religious sects brought to the country by missionaries from the United States. Many of these non-Catholic faiths blossomed first along the Caribbean coast, but most have now also spread to the western part of the country. Some of the largest are the Moravian Church, the Baptist Convention of Nicaragua, and the Assemblies of God. The

Moravian Church, for example, is the most popular religion among the Miskito Indians and others living in eastern Nicaragua. Other faiths include the Church of God, the Church of the Nazarene, the Church of Jesus Christ of Latter-day Saints (Mormons), Jehovah's Witnesses, and the Seventh-day Adventists.

POVERTY, UNEMPLOYMENT, AND CRIME

After family ties and religion, the most important fact of life for many Nicaraguans is their incessant poverty. Although a small sector of people have jobs or businesses and live middle-class lives, and a few are even wealthy landowners, Nicaragua is still the poorest country in the western hemisphere. Its poverty is marked by a low per capita income, an unemployment/underemployment rate that hovers around 50 percent, and a huge foreign debt that eats up a large chunk of the country's revenues. Over half of the Nicaraguan population lives in poverty, and at least 800,000 people live in extreme poverty, surviving on less than $1 per day. Many of the poorest Nicaraguans live in rural areas and in the eastern and central regions of the country.

The poor lack adequate food and clean water, and suffer from malnutrition, serious diseases, and chronic health problems. Children often drop out of school at an early age to try to find work. Housing for many consists of primitive shacks that lack electricity, running water, and toilets. People are forced to survive any way they can. For many, this involves working as street vendors, selling anything from food to cigarettes, or doing any kind of small job that comes along. Others have turned to selling drugs, prostitution, and other crimes, creating a high crime rate in Nicaragua and making its cities quite dangerous.

Contributing to the problem of poverty is a high birthrate that is increasing Nicaragua's population at an alarming rate. This population growth is concentrated in urban areas such as Managua, but is also a problem in rural Nicaragua. As Thomas W. Walker notes, "From 1979 to 1989 the population grew by a phenomenal 52 percent,"[19] and since then the population has continued to expand. Many mothers give birth while they are still teenagers, and one in four households are now headed by women. The family structure is often further undermined by family violence, which creates dangerous

and unhealthy environments for both children and adults. The growing population also causes increasing damage to the environment. In the cities, increased numbers of people strain the limits of the transportation and sanitation systems, and in rural Nicaragua, the poor often cut down the forests to create farmland for subsistence crops.

A poor family stands outside their home in a shantytown outside Managua. Nicaragua is the poorest nation in the Americas.

EDUCATION, HEALTH, AND HOUSING PROGRAMS

The Sandinistas began trying to address the problems of the poor as soon as they came to power. In the area of education, for example, the government launched new campaigns, increased the funding for primary and secondary education, doubled the number of teachers, and built many new schools. A 1980 literacy campaign taught over 400,000 Nicaraguans to read and write in just five months. The program quickly reduced the illiteracy rate from 50 percent to 23 percent of the total population. The literacy effort was followed up with the establishment of a program of adult basic education, and by 1984 over 200,000 people were enrolled in some 17,000 local education collectives. Enrollments at the primary, secondary, and college levels also jumped dramatically. By 1989 the total student population in Nicaragua had grown to more than 1 million.

The Contra war, the country's economic crisis, and the austerity methods employed to improve the economy, however, soon forced a reduction in education spending and

Students study Spanish grammar in a village school. Improving education was a top priority to the Sandinista government.

disrupted the country's promising education programs. The rapidly growing population has further taxed the government's ability to educate its people. Today, primary public education is free and available to most Nicaraguans, and children between six and twelve years old must attend school. Yet there is a lack of schools, books, and supplies. As a result, most students can go to school for only half a day. Teachers, too, are in short supply and turnover is high, largely because teachers are paid such low salaries by the government. Also, because of lack of family finances, only about 47 percent of students make it to the secondary level. Even fewer are able to attend college.

Health care, like education, has declined since the demise of the Sandinista government. During the Somoza era, most Nicaraguans had virtually no access to modern health care. Seeking to change this, the Sandinistas increased health care funding, reorganized the system to provide access to care for all Nicaraguans, increased the numbers of hospitals and doctors, and placed a new emphasis on primary and preventative medicine. As a result of these efforts, five new hospitals and hundreds of new health clinics were built, and thousands of community health care volunteers were mobilized for broad-based vaccination and sanitation campaigns. The early years of the Sandinista government were marked by substantial drops in infant mortality, increases in life expectancy, and reductions in cases of serious diseases. In fact, in 1983 the World Health Organization declared Nicaragua a "Model Nation in Health Attention."

Unfortunately, the country's health programs, like its education programs, deteriorated beginning in the late 1980s due to decreased funding and the effects of the Contra war. The health system had less money for medicines, supplies, and doctors' salaries at the same time that it was swamped with war victims and increased disease and illness caused by jumps in overall poverty. Today, because of the lack of government resources resulting from the country's continuing

REFUGEES FROM NICARAGUA

During the Sandinista revolution and the Contra war in Nicaragua, many thousands of Nicaraguans fled the country to escape the fighting and find a better life. Between 1979 and 1987, some estimates say that more than 140,000 Nicaraguans, or almost 5 percent of the population, left the country. Others say the figure is closer to half a million. These refugees included a third of Nicaragua's college-educated professionals, as well as many poor Nicaraguans. Many of the refugees came to the United States, where they started businesses or worked in low-paid service jobs in places like Miami, Houston, and Los Angeles. The United States granted these refugees special treatment for a time, but most were eventually turned down for asylum and some were even deported. At the end of the war and during the early 1990s, as many as 120,000 refugees returned to Nicaragua. These refugees, together with Nicaraguans who were displaced from their homes during Hurricane Mitch, created a huge burden for the Nicaraguan government, which was already struggling to provide for a large poor population. Given the country's desperate economic conditions, little was done to help the returning refugees, and many returned to the United States.

economic problems, the country still lacks sufficient doctors and hospitals and most Nicaraguans cannot afford basic health care. The hospitals and doctors that do exist are usually found in urban areas. Rural Nicaraguans often resort to faith healers and herbal medicines. As a result, the poor are dying from treatable illnesses such as pneumonia, and even completely preventable illnesses such as malaria, dysentery, and diarrhea are common due to poor sanitation and unclean water supplies.

A similar story can be told about efforts to improve housing in Nicaragua. The Sandinista government tried to remedy Nicaragua's inadequate housing by building some public housing, instituting programs to protect renters and homeowners, and providing incentives for the construction of new private housing. Like education and health care programs, however, housing initiatives soon were scaled back because of funding problems and overwhelmed by large numbers of war refugees. Today, even basic shelter remains but a dream for many Nicaraguans.

WOMEN

Women undoubtedly shoulder the heaviest burden in Nicaraguan society. In their traditional role as mothers and homemakers, they have to deal directly with the problems of poverty and worry about providing food, schooling, and health care for their children when there is little government or other support. They also are often treated as second-class citizens in a society where they receive less education, are offered fewer work opportunities, and when employed, earn less money than men. Even worse, many women in Nicaragua often suffer from domestic abuse and violence committed by their husbands, fathers, or other family members.

The Sandinistas, for their part, sought to improve the lives of women. Many women even participated in the Sandinista revolution as guerrilla fighters, fighting and dying alongside male soldiers. After coming to power, the Sandinistas encouraged women to work outside the home, placed provisions into the constitution to guarantee gender equality, and assigned women prominent positions in the Sandinista government. Yet these changes did not overturn centuries-old social and religious customs that have traditionally governed relations between the sexes in Nicaragua. At the root of these customs is an attitude of machismo (masculinity) common in Latin societies.

The machismo attitude encourages men to act assertively and to take every opportunity to demonstrate their power and masculinity. Women, meanwhile, are expected to remain dependent, submissive, and faithful. In Nicaragua, these attitudes contribute to a deep social inequality between women and men, and to continuing problems of family poverty and domestic violence. The machismo culture also leads to early sexual activities that are often practiced without contraception. At the same time, the continuing influence of the Roman Catholic Church has kept abortion illegal in Nicaragua. These social conditions are largely responsible for the country's high birthrate, and for an increasing number of poor, young, single mothers who are forced to find work to support their families. These women often come home from their outside work and perform all the domestic chores in their households, a situation

Female soldiers in the Sandinista army assemble for a drill. The Sandinistas actively recruited women to participate in the revolution.

THE NICARAGUAN WOMEN'S MOVEMENT

The struggle to advance women's equality in Nicaragua began with the 1979 Sandinista revolution. Under the Sandinista government, women were provided with education, health care, and other improvements in their lives. When the government changed hands in 1990, however, these programs were ended and the Chamorro government enacted policies that denied health care to the poor, restricted birth control, and provided help only to traditional two-parent families.

In the 1990s, however, a number of Nicaraguan feminists gained prominence and helped create a growing women's movement. The movement was formed from many loosely co-ordinated women's groups who work together to promote causes and legislation beneficial to women. These groups have been successful in several areas. For example, they helped re-vise the penal code to make domestic violence a criminal act and established a network of women's police stations across the country to encourage women to report and take legal ac-tion against violent partners. In addition, the creation of a women's health network has provided some neighborhood health services through local clinics and nongovernmental or-ganizations. Slowly, the status of women in Nicaraguan society appears to be changing.

that creates a hard life of constant work for many women. Wealthier women are more likely to escape this fate, because they typically do not need to work outside the home and sometimes have domestic help for household tasks. Many poor women, however, place their hopes in the efforts of the Nicaraguan women's movement, a force that originated dur-ing the Sandinista years and continues today to fight for im-provements and help for women.

Despite the many obstacles facing the country, visitors to Nicaragua report that Nicaraguans have remained an open, friendly, and surprisingly cheerful people. As travel writers Joshua Berman and Randy Wood put it, "Nicaraguans . . . sur-vive amidst the day-to-day struggle . . . with an incredible vitality and with the ability to enjoy life in a way more pros-perous societies have forgotten."[20] They do the best they can to cope with the difficulties of their lives and continue to hope for a better future.

CULTURAL TRADITIONS

5

Throughout their many years of political and economic struggles, Nicaraguans have managed to maintain their heritage of artistic traditions. In fact, despite widespread poverty and the government's inability to provide funding, arts such as poetry and literature, music, dance, murals, and handicrafts have flourished in the country. Today, these arts traditions continue to thrive, making Nicaraguan culture rich, varied, and unique in Central America.

FESTIVALS AND HOLIDAYS

Foremost among Nicaraguans' cultural traditions is a love of festivals and celebrations. As travel writer Rodolfo Narváez puts it, "Nicaraguan people are fond of parties: This statement is an unquestionable truth."[21] Nicaragua has many national holidays, each of which provides an excuse for celebrating. These include New Year's Day, Independence Day (which honors Nicaragua's 1821 independence from Spain on September 15), Festival de San Sebastian (which honors the patron saint San Sebastian on January 20), and religious holidays (Christmas and Easter). In addition, almost every town and village has its own annual festival that attracts large local crowds. Many towns, in fact, have more than one festival each year. Most of these are religious in nature; typically, they honor a patron saint, who is celebrated with parties, processions, and other festivities.

The town of Masaya, for example, has one of the longest and most popular festivals in Nicaragua honoring the patron saint Jerónimo. The festival begins on September 20 when a statue of the saint is taken from its altar, elaborately decorated with flowers, and carried throughout the town. This procession is followed by many townspeople and is accompanied by the sounds of music, bells, fireworks, and singing. The festivities continue for many weeks and do not end until the first week of December. This festival period is characterized by lots of music and dancing in the streets,

A man dressed as a woman carrying a jug atop her head parades with other revelers through the streets of Masaya during the festival of Saint Jerónimo.

local food delicacies accompanied by rum and beer, and various organized presentations. Often, these presentations feature popular folkloric dances and comedy skits that make fun of the original Spanish conquerors. They also include a huge mass held on September 30 at the local church. Close to fifty thousand worshippers from all over Nicaragua travel to Masaya to attend the mass and to pray to the saint for their own personal miracles.

One of the most important celebrations for Catholics, however, is December 8, when the Immaculate Conception of the Virgin Mary, or Purísima, is celebrated for an entire week. Purísima is far more important to Nicaraguans than other holidays, including Christmas. Lidiana, a young girl from Nicaragua, describes the typical Purísima celebration:

It is something like Halloween. People go from house to house singing songs that are like Christmas carols during Christmas, and people give them fruits, candy, toys, etc. Images are put up all over and lights are put up around them. People also have praying ceremonies in houses, followed by a party where the host gives out mugs of hot "pinolillo," a traditional drink, and toys, candy, fruits, fudge, and most important of all, a single firecracker, to be let out at midnight. At that time, thousands of firecrackers go up at the same time and a display of lights go up in the sky. There is also a lot of booms, bangs, pops, and taps from the sky. It is breathtaking.[22]

The city of León, in particular, is known for its Purísima celebrations. An evening mass is held on December 7 and attended by Catholics from all over Central America. Afterward, the León Cathedral bells ring, people set off fireworks, and partygoers celebrate on the streets all night long. Purísima is followed by two other important religious holidays: Christmas, or Navidad, and Easter, or Pascua. Most Nicaraguans also celebrate the week before Easter, a time known as Holy Week, or Semana Santa.

MUSIC AND DANCE

Music and dancing are always at the center of Nicaraguan celebrations. Traditional Indian folk music and dances, in particular, are very popular. Unlike in many surrounding countries in Central America, which have largely abandoned native traditions, Nicaraguans respect and continue to practice these indigenous customs. As travel writer Paul Glassman describes, "In Nicaragua, not only are traditional dances that are rooted in pre-Hispanic customs dusted off and trotted out at town fiestas, they are preserved and practiced and encouraged in folkloric dance groups, and taught to kids as after-school activities, along with aerobics and ballet."[23] Traditional dancers often wear grotesque masks, hats, and costumes, and inevitably they play out a story line. A common theme reenacts the Spanish conquest in a comedic or unflattering way.

Traditional dances are usually performed to music played on the marimba, an instrument similar to a xylophone. The marimba has bars made of rosewood that are struck with a mallet, or hammer, to make rich, mellow tones. In Nicaragua, the marimba is usually played by a sitting performer who holds the instrument on his knees. The marimba is often accompanied by other instruments such as a bass fiddle, guitar, or mandolin. Marimba music is widely played at festivals and many other social functions.

Modern music, too, is an integral part of everyday life in Nicaragua. As Hazel Plunkett explains, "Wherever you go in Nicaragua, there is likely to be music . . . the sounds of well-worn recordings blast from makeshift homes, market stalls, and rickety buses. On Saturday evenings bars and dance halls fill with people eager to dance."[24] In the western part of the country, the beat of salsa music is common, while in the east, reggae and calypso are more popular. In fact, Bluefields, the largely English-speaking town on the Caribbean coast, is known as a center for reggae music. Other music popular with Nicaraguans includes Cuban, Brazilian, Mexican, and Panamanian performers, as well as pop stars from Europe and the United States. In addition, the small Garifuna community in eastern Nicaragua is known for its own, indigenous brand of popular music.

NICARAGUAN FOOD

Like music and dance, food is also an important part of any Nicaraguan celebration. Because of their poverty, many Nicaraguans cannot afford to regularly eat meat, so beans serve as the main source of protein. In fact, one of the most common dishes eaten by Nicaraguans is *gallo pinto*, or "painted rooster," which is basically rice and beans spiced with garlic, onions, and sometimes cheese. It is often eaten for breakfast and served with eggs and cabbage and tomato salad. Corn is also a dietary staple in Nicaragua. Like Mexicans and other Central Americans, Nicaraguans use corn to make foods such as tortillas, tamales, and enchiladas. Unlike in some other Latin cultures, however, Nicaraguans usually do not season their food with hot chilies.

Other traditional dishes include *bajo* (a slowly cooked mix of meat, a banana-like fruit called plantains, and vegetables), *nacatamales* (meat and vegetables wrapped in leaves from a pungent banana-like plant), *vigoron* (pork rinds, cabbage, and cassava, a starchy food made from the roots of the cassava plant), and *mondongo* (tripe and beef knuckles). Typical desserts in Nicaragua include *arroz de leche* (rice pudding), flan (caramel pudding), and *pío quinto* (rum cake).

In Caribbean coastal areas, however, typical dishes are quite different from those in the west. Here, dishes such as coconut stew, fish, lobster, and other fresh seafood are the dietary mainstays. For those who can afford it, Nicaragua's cities also offer a fairly wide variety of international food as well as fast-food-chain fare.

Nicaraguans also enjoy a vast array of exotic tropical fruits, such as mangos, papayas, tamarind, *jocotes* (similar to small mangos), *guayabas* (guavas), *pitaya* (cactus fruit), and *melocoton* (star fruit). These tropical fruits are often used to make popular local drinks called *frescos*. Other local beverages include *tis* (a unique drink made from corn and cacao) and the country's delicious coffee. Some of the best Nicaraguan coffee comes from the mountain areas around the town of Matagalpa. Most Nicaraguans who can afford it drink their coffee with lots of milk for breakfast and black, sweetened with sugar, during the rest of the day. Typical alcoholic drinks popular with Nicaraguans are the traditional *chichi* (made from fermented corn mash) and locally produced beers and rum. Nicaragua's rum, a brand called Flor de Caña (Flower of the Cane), is said by many to be the best in all of Latin America.

Children enjoy a plate of gallo pinto, *a traditional Nicaraguan dish.*

GETTING AROUND IN NICARAGUA

Unlike in more developed countries, Nicaragua's dilapidated transportation systems make traveling around the country somewhat difficult. Roads near the capital city of Managua are in fairly good condition. They are paved and usually have two lanes, although they may sometimes become congested. Old school buses provide slow, uncomfortable, yet cheap transportation around urban areas. North of León, conditions get worse and roads, although often paved, are usually in bad shape with numerous potholes. Along the Pacific coast, one encounters dirt roads, and anywhere in the mountains or in the Caribbean region of Nicaragua a four-wheel-drive vehicle is necessary because most roads are narrow, deeply rutted, dirt trails. Travel to these more remote parts of Nicaragua is best done by air. Several small local airlines fly regularly from Managua to places such

as the Caribbean coast and the Corn Islands. In addition, in parts of the country near lakes, rivers, or oceans, people often travel by motorboat.

Nicaraguans wait to board a bus at a crowded bus stop in Managua.

POETRY AND LITERATURE

Along with celebrations featuring music, dance, and food, one of Nicaragua's most beloved cultural traditions is poetry and writing. In fact, poetry has a long heritage in Nicaragua as an honorable and exalted art. As journalist Margaret Randall explains, "Throughout Nicaraguan culture, the poet is the high priest. The prophet. The maker of visions. The singer of songs. The one who knows and can say it for others the way others feel it but cannot say it for themselves."[25]

One of Nicaragua's earliest and most famous poets was Rubén Darío (1867–1916). Darío became known around the world as the founder of a new Spanish literary movement called modernism, a lively form of poetry that used free verse, symbolism, and rhythm to convey its message. Although Darío lived outside of Nicaragua for most of his life, he returned to visit often and was a very effective diplomat for his country. His poetry expressed his great love of his homeland and made Nicaragua very proud. He is still revered as one of Nicaragua's greatest historical and literary figures.

Darío was followed in the twentieth century by many other poets and writers who have kept Nicaragua's rich literary traditions very much alive. Many of these were warrior-poets who became leaders in Nicaragua's Sandinista revolution. One such poet was Ernesto Cardenal, a Catholic priest and revolutionary who joined the FSLN and later became Nicaragua's minister of culture. In this position, he helped stimulate a revival of the arts in Nicaragua during the early years of the Sandinista government. Cardenal is no longer involved in politics but remains an active supporter of the arts. Another of the country's most distinguished and prolific writers is novelist Sergio Ramírez. Like Cardenal, Ramírez supported the Sandinista revolution. He was elected Nicaragua's vice president 1984. Over his long career, he has written more than thirty books, many of them about the revolution, and he still lives and writes in Nicaragua.

Nicaragua has also produced female writers. Today, one of the best-known women writers from Nicaragua is Gioconda Belli, a strong feminist who has written several books of poetry, three novels, and nonfiction pieces. Belli, who now lives in the United States, is known for her bold style of writing and controversial topics. For example, her famous first novel, *The Inhabited Woman*, concerns a woman who abandons her traditional female role to become a guerrilla fighter in the Sandinista revolution. In 1998 Belli continued this controversial style by publishing an interview with the stepdaughter of Sandinista leader Daniel Ortega about her surprising allegations of sexual abuse against her stepfather. One of Belli's most recent books is a memoir about her life called *The Country Under My Skin*, in which she describes the effects of Nicaragua's social and political upheaval on her personal life.

NEWSPAPERS, RADIO, AND TELEVISION

Another form of writing, journalism, has been used mainly as a political weapon by partisan groups from both ends of the political spectrum in Nicaragua. Press freedoms did not exist during the Somoza years. The Sandinistas also controlled some parts of the media, including television programming. And on at least one occasion the Sandinista government shut down the newspaper *La Prensa*.

MANY DIFFERENT VIEWPOINTS

Today, freedom of speech is guaranteed by the Nicaraguan constitution, and there is no state censorship of the media. A number of newspapers exist and they publish many different viewpoints. Most newspapers still have political affiliations with one political party or another. One example is the conservative newspaper *La Prensa*, which has been operated since 1926 by the Chamorros, the family of Nicaraguan president Violeta Chamorro. During her presidency, however, the editorial staff of the newspaper rebelled against the control by the president's daughter and sought to become more independent in its outlook. Two other ma-

CULTURE IN GRANADA AND LEÓN

The Nicaraguan cities of León and Granada contain many of Nicaragua's cultural landmarks. León lies just north of the capital city of Managua. It is one of Nicaragua's oldest cities, founded in 1524. León's main attraction is its old Metropolitan Cathedral, the largest in Central America and a marvel of colonial architecture. The cathedral houses artistic masterpieces and is the burial site for Nicaragua's beloved poet Rubén Darío. In addition, León is home to a university and law school and has long been a site of political battles and revolution. It was here, in 1956, that President Somoza was gunned down, and many Sandinista leaders hailed from the city.

Granada, located on the shores of Lake Nicaragua, was also founded in the 1500s by the Spanish and contains fine examples of colonial architecture. Two of its architectural gems are La Merced Church, built in 1543, and Xalteva Church, which dates to the early seventeenth century. Granada, too, has a long history of political activism, mostly as a conservative rival to the more liberal León. Together, Granada and León have long served as the main political, cultural, and religious centers of Nicaragua.

LA PRENSA

SIN LIBERTAD DE PRENSA NO HAY LIBERTAD

jor daily newspapers, *El Nuevo Diario* and *Barricada*, were historically known as pro-Sandinista papers. These papers, however, have since become more independent of the FSLN. None of Nicaragua's newspapers, however, have huge circulation numbers, because the poor simply cannot afford to buy them.

Radio, another form of media, is much more accessible to the general public. As social scientist Nina Serafino explains, "The greatest news source for most Nicaraguans is the radio."[26] In fact, some radio stations have been considered so politically influential among the Nicaraguan public that opponents of their political positions have physically attacked them. A conservative radio station, Radio Corporación, for example, was hit twice by the Sandinistas in the early years of the Chamorro government. Radio also provides an important source of music and cultural information. Today, there are more than one hundred radio stations in the country. Radio Corporación continues to broadcast as a voice for the most conservative members of the UNO coalition. Other influential stations include Radio Nicaragua, a government-run station, and Radio Ya, one of

Demonstrators hold a sign that reads "Without freedom of the press there is no freedom" in protest of the Sandinista suppression of the newspaper La Prensa *in 1986.*

the country's most popular stations run by supporters of the Sandinistas.

Television remains less important than radio in Nicaragua, since many poor people cannot afford TVs. Although growing in popularity and influence, television is still largely limited to wealthier Nicaraguans and those who live in urban areas. Managua, for example, has three television stations that broadcast both cable and local programming. During Sandinista rule, television stations were completely controlled by the government, which sought to promote local programming and public access. Today, little of this local Nicaraguan content remains. Instead, Nicaraguan television broadcasts a lot of partisan political information and a significant number of foreign programs. Nicaraguans especially love soap operas broadcast from neighboring Latin countries and American cartoons and movies.

Other news sources such as the Internet are not yet widely available or used in Nicaragua. Indeed, many Nicaraguans still do not even have telephone lines, the necessary ingredient for the basic dial-up Internet service. The latest available information (from 1996), for example, shows only 140,000 telephone lines in service out of a population of more than 5 million. As is the case with television, only the wealthier people can afford these advanced technological tools. However, the Internet is slowly becoming more widespread in the country, as increasing numbers of businesses, individuals, and nongovernmental organizations are going online to promote their products, services, and activities.

CRAFTS, MURALS, AND MODERN ART

In addition to the written word, Nicaragua has also produced many visual artists and craftspeople. Traditional craft items, such as pottery and masks, are still made and sold. The village of San Juan de Oriente, for example, has been known for its pottery for hundreds of years. Today, it is the site of a large pottery cooperative and many family-run workshops. The pottery produced here includes traditional pre-Columbian images as well as more contemporary geometric and floral designs.

Nicaragua, too, is home to many painters. The Archipiélago de Solentiname, a group of islands located in the southern part of Lake Nicaragua, is the site of a society of artists established in the 1970s by the poet and former minister of culture, Ernesto Cardenal. The Sandinista government, under Cardenal's leadership, encouraged local fishermen and others in this area to paint, and their artwork soon became known as a colorful, primitive style of painting called *Escuela Primitivista de Solentiname*. This style featured rural scenes from Nicaraguans' daily life as well as portraits of revolutionary heroes and other liberation and religious themes. Portraits of the revolutionary poet Sandino, for example, were common.

Thereafter, the primitive style became very popular in Nicaragua. Political and other murals appeared on walls

MARKETPLACES AND SHOPPING

Nicaragua, unlike some other Central American countries, has few large shopping centers or malls and imports few products from other countries. Instead, shopping in Nicaragua often means buying locally made or produced items from individual craftspeople or from small shops. In fact, many towns in Nicaragua specialize in one product or another. In the town of

Masaya, for example, items such as clothing, leatherwork, wood crafts, and baskets can be found. In San Juan de Oriente, reproductions of pre-Columbian pottery are the main product. Other towns have their specialties as well. For example, León sells embroidered shirts; Estelí, leather furniture; San Juan de Limay, white stone carvings; and Diriamba, dolls and seashell creations. Nicaragua's largest city, Managua, sells local products from all parts of the country.

Displaying her baskets high atop her head, a woman standing in a Masaya road waits to make a sale.

throughout the country. Primitive artists also were recognized internationally. They were able to sell their paintings in major cities such as New York and Paris. Today, colorful murals still adorn many large walls and buildings in Nicaraguan cities. Murals are especially prominent in the university town of León.

SPORTS

Yet another highly popular pastime in Nicaragua is sports. Unlike many other Latin countries, however, where soccer rules as the favorite sport, Nicaragua prefers baseball. American marines, who occupied the country for many years, are believed to have brought the sport to Nicaragua, where it became a national obsession. As reporter Jay Feldman puts it, "To say that Nicaraguans are crazy for baseball is a monumental understatement. . . . Baseball is a passion in Nicaragua, a profound expression of the national character."[27]

Today, throughout Nicaragua both boys and girls use sticks or whatever equipment they can find to play baseball games on any available parcel of ground. Organized teams also compete, sometimes with great success. In the 1996 Olympic Games, Nicaragua's national team, *La Selección*, almost won a bronze medal, and in 1998 the team came in third in the World Championships held in Italy. Nicaraguan baseball players have sometimes been good enough to make it into professional baseball leagues. The country's most famous athlete, for example, is Dennis Martínez, a Nicaraguan baseball player who became the most successful Latin American pitcher in the U.S. Major Leagues. In Nicaragua, Martínez is treated as a national hero. His fans call him *El Presidente* as a result of rumors that he was planning to return to Nicaragua and enter politics.

Nicaragua's second most popular sport is boxing. Those who have great ability in this sport sometimes achieve great riches. Two Nicaraguans, in fact, rose from poverty to become world champions. Alexis Arguello won three world titles in the 1970s, and Rosendo Álvarez followed a similar path in the 1990s. Football, although much less popular than baseball or boxing, is also enjoyed by some Nicaraguans.

Nicaragua clearly can be proud of its unique and fascinating culture. Because of its poverty and turbulent history, the country is only slowly entering the modern world of technology and development. Yet it may be this very delay of modern influences that has allowed the country's vibrant cultural traditions to endure and thrive in contemporary Nicaragua.

In 1998 Nicaraguan Dennis Martínez (in dark jacket) is honored by his Atlanta Braves teammates. Baseball is Nicaragua's most popular sport.

6

Nicaragua's Future

Nicaragua still faces formidable hurdles in its struggle to develop as an independent, democratic nation. The country's economy remains weak, which makes it difficult to alleviate the bitter poverty that has gripped Nicaraguans for so long. At the same time, Nicaragua finds its fragile environment threatened and its relatively new democracy eroded by corruption and greed. Despite these many challenges, many observers think the country's future may be hopeful. Nicaragua has finally emerged from the long Somoza nightmare, and its deep national pride and resilient people give it great strength.

ECONOMIC ISSUES

Despite its recent embrace of democracy, Nicaragua remains one of the world's poorest and least developed countries. Its biggest task thus continues to be building and stabilizing its economy. Fortunately, the country has made some progress in this area in recent years. Thanks largely to prudent economic policies pursued by President Bolaños since his election in 2001, inflation has been significantly reduced, budget deficits have been declining, and foreign investments have increased to more than $150 million annually. Agricultural products (mainly coffee but also cotton, sugar, meat, sesame, and bananas), as well as seafood and gold, continue to be Nicaragua's most important exports, but recently its greatest economic success has been in the tourism industry, which constituted the country's main source of foreign income in 2003.

In addition, in 2004 President Bolaños secured major debt relief from multinational creditors such as the United States, Russia, and Australia. Altogether, under agreements negotiated by the IMF and World Bank, various countries pledged to forgive approximately 73 percent of Nicaragua's debt, cutting about $4.5 billion from what had been a $6.5 billion debt and reducing the country's annual debt payments from $500 million to as little as $170 million. Such relief places Nicaragua in a much better financial position. The debt reduction makes the country more stable and attractive to foreign investors, and this should help to promote stronger economic growth.

Nevertheless, the economy's annual growth rate of 1.5 to 3 percent of its gross domestic product (GDP) is still too low to run the country effectively and at the same time pay back Nicaragua's remaining foreign debts. Debt payments continue to take money from projects that are desperately needed to boost Nicaragua's economy and help the Nicaraguan people. As President Bolaños has complained, "Debt hinders my presidency because it absorbs funds that should be destined for roads, health, and education."[28] Indeed, the 2004 debt relief, although greatly appreciated, was less helpful than some expected, largely because Nicaragua had already not been paying the full amount that it owed on the debt. Under the new debt terms, however, the country

President Bolaños (left) meets with the Italian ambassador to discuss debt relief. Debt relief has been a tremendous boon to Nicaragua's economy.

will pay less than what it was paying before, and this will free up government revenues that can then be spent on Nicaraguans instead of for debt payments. Nevertheless, Nicaragua is expected in the near future to remain dependent on international aid and debt relief.

Yet in the long run, many experts predict that Nicaragua will likely succeed in its efforts to improve its economy. The very fact that the country is so underdeveloped, analysts say, makes it ripe for investments. It has cheap labor to attract industry and unspoiled ecological riches that provide a perfect setting for tourism. Further more, Nicaragua's leaders are taking aggressive steps to promote these assets. The Nicaraguan Tourism Institute, for example, began a massive new campaign known as "Come Try Nicaragua" to air on international cable channel CNN's Headline News in 2005. The goal of the ads is to portray the country as business

THE NICARAGUAN CANAL PROPOSAL

One of the ideas for economic development in Nicaragua is a proposal for an interocean transportation route that would either take the form of a coast-to-coast rail line or include both water canals and a railroad line. The project, often called the "Dry Canal," would compete with the Panama Canal by providing a second route to transport goods between the Caribbean Sea and the Pacific Ocean. Advocates claim that the project will create at least twenty thousand construction jobs, employ six thousand to seven thousand workers to operate the facilities after construction, and attract additional economic development along the route and at its seaports. Environmentalists, however, caution that such development would cause great harm to the environment. On the Caribbean side, industrial development would lead to large-scale deforestation of rain forests, damage fragile coral reefs, and jeopardize marine creatures. On the Pacific side, development would threaten one of the last remaining tropical dry forests as well as rich coastal areas. In addition, an east-west canal would prohibit the creation of a north-to-south Central American biological corridor that environmentalists hope will conserve nature and provide large animals the space they need to survive. The canal idea today continues to be controversial.

friendly to attract more foreign investment. Moreover, after years of political dictatorship, Nicaragua's democratic government promises at last to provide the political stability that will attract investors. Because of these strengths, some experts expect Nicaragua to soon become one of Latin America's fastest growing economies.

POVERTY AND SOCIAL ISSUES

Experts say that a large part of the country's economic development must include social programs to alleviate the poverty and unemployment that is still rampant among Nicaragua's people. Although overall poverty in Nicaragua fell slightly from 50.3 percent of the population in 1993 to 45.8 percent in 2001, the population growth has resulted in a net increase in the numbers of poor Nicaraguans. Today, these figures mean that millions still live with insufficient food, in poor sanitary conditions, and without access to health care, adequate housing, or a decent education. Even worse, extreme poverty in Nicaragua continues to be a problem, especially in central urban parts of Managua and rural areas. In these areas, according to the World Bank, over 25 percent of the population struggles to survive on less than one dollar a day. At this income, people are often unable to get enough food to meet the minimum daily caloric requirement (defined as 2,226 calories per adult) considered necessary for a healthy life. For the poor facing such horrific conditions, as Jesuit volunteers Rachel Mahlik and Marvin Grilliot explain, "prospects for living a life with dignity are bleak."[29]

The societal effects of Nicaragua's terrible poverty are staggering. One out of every three children suffers from chronic malnutrition, and many mothers and children die during childbirth because of lack of medical care. Large numbers of children are forced to work instead of going to school. And families are slowly disintegrating due to high rates of teen pregnancies, increased numbers of households headed by a single parent, primarily the mother, and rising family violence. In addition, drug use and crime rates have skyrocketed, along with the risk of HIV infections, making life even more unsafe.

To reverse this grim reality, experts say the Nicaraguan people must be provided with education and jobs. Studies,

Hungry children wait for a soup kitchen in Managua to open. A large percentage of Nicaragua's children suffer from malnutrition.

for example, have shown that there is a strong correlation between education and economic well-being. Yet in Nicaragua one out of every two children drops out of school before the fifth grade. Increasing government spending on education, therefore, is key to resolving the country's long-term cycle of poverty.

For the more immediate future, experts advise that job creation is essential. During the Sandinista rule, public works projects succeeded in putting many poor people to work on projects that also benefited the country by improving infrastructure such as roads, bridges, and public buildings. In Nicaragua today, free-trade policies are favored. Under these policies, foreign businesses set up shops in Nicaragua to take advantage of its cheap labor. For the poor, this provides much-needed work, but some critics complain that many of these local businesses are nothing more than sweatshops that exploit the poor by paying extremely low wages while earning handsome profits for their foreign owners. Many of these businesses, for example, are Asian-owned textile shops that pay little to workers but export their clothes to the United States at high prices. The challenge for

Nicaragua's leaders, therefore, will be guiding economic policy to create decent jobs while continuing to attract foreign investment.

Another part of the challenge of reducing poverty in Nicaragua, many observers say, involves improving the unequal distribution of land. In a country that is still largely dependent on agriculture, landownership often determines a person's wealth and economic well-being. With land, rural peasants can generate income by selling agricultural products on the open market, or at least grow enough food to feed themselves and their families. Without land, peasants are often left unemployed and in deep poverty. Many of these rural poor, desperate to survive, crowd into Nicaragua's cities to find work, creating large slums. Twenty years after the Sandinistas' land reforms, however, the country is now seeing a reversal of reforms and the rebirth of large landholdings. Much of Nicaragua's best lands are now owned by foreigners and sometimes corrupt government officials, while the number of poor landless peasants is increasing. Policies to address these inequities, some argue, are central to an effective antipoverty program in Nicaragua.

To alleviate the conditions of disease, mortality, and hopelessness that accompany poverty, experts claim that government funds must also be spent on providing basic health care, nutrition, water and sanitation, and other services to Nicaragua's poor. Progress must be made in improving other infrastructure as well, such as providing electricity to poor families and providing paved roads and other transportation systems to allow people to travel to work, school, and health facilities.

In 2001 Nicaragua, the IMF, and the World Bank agreed to a plan that incorporated many elements geared toward poverty reduction. Called the Strengthened Growth and Poverty Reduction Strategy (SGPRS), the plan set an ambitious goal of cutting Nicaragua's poverty in half by 2015. Assessments by the IMF in January 2004, however, suggested that Nicaragua's progress in achieving the goals set out in its antipoverty plan has so far been disappointing.

Whether Nicaragua can truly address its deep poverty problems by increasing government spending, and at the same time pay off its remaining loans, keep a lid on the budget deficit, and invest in the economy, seems uncertain at best. Many in Nicaragua hope that a rising economy will eventually improve the lives of all the population.

ENVIRONMENTAL CONCERNS

Yet another urgent problem in need of funding and attention is the rapid degradation of Nicaragua's environment. The country's forests, in particular, are being lost at an alarming rate. According to environmental groups, 50 percent of the forest cover has disappeared since 1950, and today the rate of deforestation is so high that Nicaragua could lose all of its remaining rain forests within ten to fifteen years if action is not taken soon. The principal cause of deforestation is economic. Landless peasants clear sections of rain forest for farmland in an effort to grow crops to survive. They plant crops for a few years until the soil runs out of nutrients and then move on to clear a new patch of forest. As Nicaraguan environment minister Auturo Harding puts it, "Poverty is the leading cause of environmental destruction [in Nicaragua]."[30] Cattle ranching and logging by large-scale commercial companies are also contributing to the problem.

Environmentalists argue that protecting the rain forests is critical in order to ensure the continuation of one of the earth's last remaining sources of rich biodiversity, where great numbers of animal, plant, and insect species exist side-by-side in one small nation. Indeed, Nicaragua has the largest remaining rain forest in Central America, and protecting its forests is key to global rain forest preservation. Strong actions are necessary, advocates say, to save the earth's wildness for human appreciation, to help absorb carbon dioxide produced by human habitation, and to preserve species for future scientific studies that could lead to cures for diseases or many other products useful to humankind.

Preventing further deforestation is also important for other reasons. Experts say, for example, that deforestation exacerbates Nicaragua's disasters (including earthquakes, volcanic eruptions, floods, and drought). In 1998 Hurricane Mitch resulted in severe floods and landslides in Nicaragua that occurred mainly in regions with steep slopes that had been denuded of their forest cover. Further loss of forests will make Nicaragua even more vulnerable to such destruc-

NICARAGUA AND THE UNITED STATES

The United States has long exercised a strong influence in Nicaragua, and it continues to do so today. Following the FSLN's loss in the 1990 elections, the United States lifted its trade embargo against the country and announced an aid package for the Chamorro government. In exchange for this aid, U.S. officials expected Nicaragua to adopt free-market reforms and to follow the economic advice offered by international economic institutions such as the International Monetary Fund. Since then, Nicaragua has largely complied with U.S. and IMF economic demands, and the United States has continued its support of Nicaragua. Today, the tie with the United States is Nicaragua's most important foreign relationship. In addition to its role as a source of aid and the country's main trading partner, the United States is home to about 1 million Nicaraguans. These foreign nationals live and work in America and send money home to relatives in Nicaragua. The funds they transfer home are a big part of Nicaragua's income. As a result of their country's continuing dependence on U.S. economic help, Nicaraguan leaders try hard to maintain good relations with the United States.

tion. Also, many of Nicaragua's indigenous peoples still live in the nation's remaining rain forests. Thus, protecting Nicaragua's forests is necessary to ensure that these cultures survive.

For a brief period, Nicaragua tried to address deforestation and related environmental issues. The Sandinista government, after it took office in 1979, implemented environmental protection laws, began reforestation programs, banned many dangerous pesticides, and established nature reserves. Two of Nicaragua's largest reserves are Bosawas, in the northeast, and the Indio-Maiz Biosphere Reserve, in the southeastern part of the country. The Sandinista land reforms were also quite helpful to forest preservation. By awarding over 5 million acres (2 million ha) of farmland to the country's peasants, the government halted the migration of poor people into the rain forests. As photojournalist Paul Jeffrey explains, "The rate of deforestation of Nicaragua's tropical rainforests dropped from 386 square miles (999 sq. km) per year in the late 1970s—the highest rate in the region—to 194 square miles (502 sq. km) by 1985—one of the region's lowest rates. This dramatic reduction in rainforest destruction was unprecedented."[31] The Sandinista efforts, however, came to an end during the Contra war, when government attention and funds were directed to the military. After the Contra war ended, the Sandinista government awarded plots of land in the rain forest to ex-Contras and government soldiers in an attempt to get them to lay down their arms. Later, as Nicaragua's economy worsened, poor peasants once again began clearing forestland to create farms. These events resulted in renewed deforestation that has continued to the present.

Today, there is an urgent need to resume environmental protections. Experts say this requires government funding and the enforcement of environmental laws, as well as solutions to the social and economic problems that cause the

A farmer rides past his cattle on a nature preserve in northeastern Nicaragua. Such preserves help to protect some of Nicaragua's forests from deforestation.

environmental damage. However, environmental concerns also compete with perhaps the even more urgent need of building the country's economy, an effort that often succeeds only by damaging the environment. One such conflict has emerged around the Bolaños government's promotion of a new interocean transportation route along the Río San Juan in southern Nicaragua. Such a project, environmental advocates claim, would be an environmental disaster. It would destroy large sections of pristine rain forest and bring more people and pollution into these rural areas. Experts hope that new, environmentally friendly development projects, such as ecotourism and sustainable agriculture, will enable Nicaragua to both save the environment and create economic growth.

CORRUPTION AND DEMOCRACY

In the end, however, Nicaragua will be able to move forward on solutions to its problems only if it elects ethical leaders who are committed to advancing the best hopes of the Nicaraguan people. Yet Nicaragua today is dealing with scandals of corruption in its government that are damaging the public's trust and support and undermining the country's focus on critical national issues. Corruption has historically plagued Nicaraguan politics. The Somoza regimes were corrupt, and since the revolution, rumors of political corruption have surfaced repeatedly over the years. In addition, despite the country's bleak poverty, governmental officials were often routinely paid salaries of $20,000 to $30,000 per month; in comparison, schoolteachers were allotted a measly $80 to $100 a month.

In recent years, however, corruption was found to have infected even the highest levels of the government. Nicaraguan president Arnoldo Alemán was accused of using public funds to build up his personal wealth and of running up a tab in personal expenses on a government credit card. Altogether, Alemán and his associates reportedly stole approximately $97.5 million from the Nicaraguan treasury. Much of this money was aid sent from other nations to help the country recover from Hurricane Mitch. Alemán's greed and lack of concern for Nicaragua's welfare was especially loathsome considering the country's deep poverty and how desperately it needed the funds.

Thanks largely to the efforts of current president Bolaños, Alemán was sentenced to twenty years in prison for money laundering, fraud, and embezzlement, among other charges. Bolaños campaigned on a platform of rooting out government corruption, and although he was Alemán's vice president, to the surprise of many he aggressively prosecuted Alemán once his crimes were uncovered. At a public meeting where Nicaragua's attorney general outlined the charges against Alemán, Bolaños expressed his outrage, saying, "Arnoldo, I never dreamed you would betray your people like this. You took pensions from the retirees, medicine from the sick, salaries from the teachers. You stole the people's trust."[32] To secure Alemán's conviction, Bolaños had to get the National Assembly to lift the immunity granted to Alemán (for being a lifetime member of the legislature), a difficult feat since many legislators still had ties to Alemán. Bolaños also made it his goal to push for legal reforms to bring greater openness to the government and to provide better management of government funds. He was successful in achieving some of these reforms. Laws were passed, for example, to strengthen controls on the use of public funds and to change the civil service system to make it more merit based.

Although greatly respected abroad, Bolaños's efforts on corruption eventually lost him support both with the Nicaraguan public and within his own Liberal Constitutionalist Party. Bolaños's anticorruption campaign awoke a sleeping Nicaraguan electorate, which now seems to distrust all politicians. A February 2004 citizens' march in Managua illustrated the public's continuing deep concern over this issue. Also, Bolaños's attack on Alemán alienated many liberal legislators who once supported him, and the liberals have joined forces with Sandinista legislators to thwart Bolaños whenever possible. Nicaragua's government, for example, is investigating the source of funding for Bolaños's 2001 campaign, trying to taint him with corruption claims. Legislators also have sought to strip Bolaños of his immunity from criminal prosecution and may even try to amend the constitution to allow Bolaños to be impeached and removed from office. As of early 2005, therefore, President Bolaños had lost most of his power to make permanent corruption reforms and was fighting just to stay in office. The resulting

political crisis has created instability that jeopardizes foreign aid and debt relief that the country so desperately needs, and may pave the way for a Sandinista comeback.

A Sandinista win in the 2006 elections, some analysts say, could create more problems for Nicaragua. Daniel Ortega, the likely Sandinista candidate for president, has himself been rumored to have engaged in corruption and has also recently been accused of sexually molesting his stepdaughter. Furthermore, Ortega is remembered by the United States as a Socialist leader who has always been hostile to U.S. power and dominance in Central America. This could create problems in Nicaragua's relations with not only the United States but also the IMF and other world economic bodies, which are greatly influenced by U.S. opinion and policies. Nicaragua's path of IMF-influenced and -funded economic and social reforms therefore might be hurt by the election of Ortega.

Political observers also point to other threats to Nicaragua's young democracy. During Alemán's presidency, for example, Ortega and Alemán made a power-sharing pact in 2000 that rewrote the electoral laws to strengthen their two

Demonstrators protest government corruption in Managua in 2002. Rooting out corruption has been an ongoing struggle in Nicaraguan politics.

NICARAGUA'S POVERTY REDUCTION PLAN

In 2001 Nicaragua, the IMF, and the World Bank agreed to a poverty reduction plan called the Strengthened Growth and Poverty Reduction Strategy (SGPRS). Strategies included enhancing economic growth; investing in education and health services; providing public services for the poor; and improving government efficiency and effectiveness. New programs to enhance education, health, and nutrition and to upgrade roads and water services were projected to cost about $230 million per year. Funding was to come from foreign aid and monies freed up from debt relief.

In 2004 the IMF said Nicaragua's progress on this plan was slow. Although reviewers praised Nicaraguan leaders for following IMF recommendations, reducing budget deficits, and addressing government corruption, the IMF noted that economic growth remained slow. The IMF also found no improvement in the conditions of poverty and little progress in areas such as education or health care. The IMF recommended that Nicaragua focus on urgent needs, such as education and health care for women, access to safe water, sanitation, electricity, roads, and land reforms. Access to safe water, the IMF said, was especially important to prevent malnutrition, diarrhea, and death among young children.

In 2004 Nicaraguan president Bolaños (right) and Florida governor Jeb Bush greet the press as the two meet to promote commerce between Nicaragua and Florida.

parties. This pact, analysts say, makes it more difficult for smaller political parties to be elected to the presidency or Nicaragua's legislature. Such political tinkering, according to experts, damages the strength of Nicaragua's democratic institutions.

Nicaragua clearly has much work to do, and its future may well depend on the quality of leadership that is elected over the next several elections. With good leaders and a population desperate for success, however, the country may have greater hope for its future than ever before in its history.

FACTS ABOUT NICARAGUA

GEOGRAPHY

Location: Central America, bordering both the Caribbean Sea and the Pacific Ocean, between Costa Rica and Honduras

Area: Total, 49,998 square miles (129,495 sq. km); land, 46,430 square miles (120, 254 sq. km); water, 3,568 square miles (4,241 sq. km)

Area comparative: Slightly smaller than the state of New York

Border countries: Costa Rica and Honduras

Coastline: 564 miles (907km)

Climate: Tropical in lowlands, cooler in highlands

Terrain: Extensive Atlantic coastal plains rising to central interior mountains; narrow Pacific coastal plain interrupted by volcanoes

Natural resources: Gold, silver, copper, tungsten, lead, zinc, timber, fish

Land use: Arable land, 15.94%; permanent crops, 1.94%; other, 82.12% (2001 estimate)

Natural hazards: Destructive earthquakes, volcanoes, landslides; extremely susceptible to hurricanes

PEOPLE

Population: 5,359,759 (July 2004 estimate)

Age structure: 0–14 years, 38.1% (male, 1,038,887; female, 1,001,518); 15–64 years, 58.9% (male, 1,570,494; female, 1,586,706); 65 years and over, 3% (male, 71,125; female, 91,029) (2004 estimate)

Birth rate: 25.5 births/1,000 population (2004 estimate)

Death rate: 4.54 deaths/1,000 population (2004 estimate)

Infant mortality rate: 30.15 deaths/1,000 live births (2004 estimate)

Life expectancy: Total population, 70.02 years; male, 67.99 years; female, 72.16 years (2004 estimate)

Fertility rate: 2.89 children born/woman (2004 estimate)

Ethnic groups: meztizo, 69%; white, 17%; black, 9%; Amerindian, 5%

Religions: Roman Catholic, 73%; Protestant 27%

Languages: Spanish (official), English and indigenous languages on Caribbean coast

Literacy rate for those age 15 and over: Total population, 67.5%; male, 67.2%; female, 67.8% (2003 estimate)

GOVERNMENT

Country name: Republic of Nicaragua (short form: Nicaragua)

Form of government: Democratic republic

Capital: Managua

Administrative divisions: 15 departments and 2 autonomous regions*: Atlantico Norte*, Atlantico Sur*, Boaco, Carazo, Chinandega, Chontales, Estelí, Granada, Jinotega, León, Madriz, Managua, Masaya, Matagalpa, Nueva Segovia, Río San Juan, Rivas

National holiday: Independence Day, September 15

Date of independence: September 15, 1821 (from Spain)

Constitution: January 9, 1987, with reforms in 1995 and 2000

Legal system: Civil law system; Supreme Court may review administrative acts

Suffrage: 16 years of age, universal and compulsory

Executive branch: Chief of state, President Enrique Bolaños Geyer (since January 10, 2002) (the president is both the chief of state and the head of government); Vice President Jose Rizo Castellon (since January 10, 2002); cabinet: Council of Ministers appointed by the president; elections: president and vice president elected on the same ticket by popular vote for a five-year term; election last held on November 4, 2001; next election to be held by November 2006

Legislative branch: Unicameral National Assembly, 92 seats; members are elected by proportional representation and party lists to serve five-year terms; one seat for previous president, one seat for runner-up in previous presidential election

Judicial branch: Supreme Court with 16 judges elected for five-year terms by the National Assembly

ECONOMY

Gross domestic product (GDP): $11.6 billion (2004 estimate); real growth, 2.3% (2004 estimate); GDP per capita, $2,300 (2004 estimate)

GDP composition: Agriculture, 28.9%; industry, 25.4%; services, 45.7% (2004 estimate)

Labor force: 1.91 million (2004 estimate)

Population below poverty line: approximately 50% (2001 estimate)

Unemployment rate: 22% plus considerable underemployment (2004 estimate)

Industries: Food processing, chemicals, machinery and metal products, textiles, clothing, petroleum refining and distribution, beverages, footwear, wood

Agriculture products: Coffee, bananas, sugarcane, cotton, rice, corn, tobacco, sesame, soya, beans, beef, veal, pork, poultry, dairy products

Exports: $632 million (2004 estimate)

Imports: $1.658 billion (2004 estimate)

Economic aid recipient: Substantial foreign support (2001 estimate)

Currency: Gold córdoba (NIO)

Notes

Chapter 1: Untouched Beauty

1. Paul Glassman, *Nicaragua Guide: Spectacular and Unspoiled.* Champlain, NY: Travel Line, 1996, p. 26.

2. David Close, *Nicaragua: Politics, Economics, and Society.* New York: Pinter, 1988, pp. 4–5.

3. Thomas W. Walker, *Nicaragua: The Land of Sandino*, third edition. Boulder, CO: Westview, 1991, p. 2.

Chapter 2: Nicaragua's Early Days

4. Close, *Nicaragua*, p. 11.

5. Close, *Nicaragua*, p. 13.

6. Nathan A. Haverstock and John P. Hoover, *Nicaragua in Pictures.* New York: Sterling, 1974, p. 19.

7. Walker, *Nicaragua*, p. 13.

8. Close, *Nicaragua*, p. 19.

9. Close, *Nicaragua*, p. 29.

10. Hazel Plunkett, *Nicaragua: A Guide to the People, Politics, and Culture.* New York: Interlink, 1999, p. 19.

Chapter 3: Democracy in Nicaragua

11. Walker, *Nicaragua*, p. 6.

12. Dennis Gilbert, "The Society and Its Environment," in Tim L. Merrill, ed., *Nicaragua: A Country Study.* Washington, DC: U.S. Government Printing Office, 1994, p. 104.

13. Walker, *Nicaragua*, p. 113.

14. Walker, *Nicaragua*, p. 54.

15. Plunkett, *Nicaragua*, p. 24.

16. Claudia Paguaga, "Enrique Bolaños Geyer: A Step Towards Consolidating Democracy in Nicaragua," February 2002, Revista INTER-FORUM. www.revistainterforum.com/english/articles/032502artprin_en.html.

CHAPTER 4: THE PEOPLE OF NICARAGUA

17. Gilbert, "The Society and Its Environment," p. 66.

18. Plunkett, *Nicaragua*, p. 74.

19. Walker, *Nicaragua*, p. 96.

20. Joshua Berman and Randy Wood, "Nicaragua: Why So Many Travelers Are Discovering This 'Black Sheep of Central America,'" Moon Handbooks, January 25, 2003. www.gonomad.com/market/0301/nicaraguaguide.html.

CHAPTER 5: CULTURAL TRADITIONS

21. Rodolfo Narváez, "Celebrating Life: The Bull-Deer Dance," Nicaragua's Best Guide. www.guideofnicaragua.com/Octubre/CelebratingToroVenado.html.

22. Lidiana, "Immaculate Conception/La Purisima-Nicaragua," KidLink, December 8, 1996. www.kidlink.org/KIDPROJ/MCC/mcc0338.html.

23. Glassman, *Nicaragua Guide*, p. 49.

24. Plunkett, *Nicaragua*, p. 82.

25. Quoted in Berman and Wood, "Nicaragua: Why So Many Travelers Are Discovering This 'Black Sheep of Central America.'"

26. Nina Serafino, "Government and Politics," in Merrill, *Nicaragua*, p. 181.

27. Jay Feldman, "Baseball in Nicaragua," *Whole Earth Review*, Fall 1987. www.findarticles.com/p/articles/mi_m1510/is_1987_Fall/ai_5151507.

CHAPTER 6: NICARAGUA'S FUTURE

28. Quoted in *Latin Trade*, "The Future Is Now," March 2003, p. 22.

29. Quoted in Tom Fox, "Living Nicaragua's Dubious Distinction," *National Catholic Reporter*, August 28, 2003. www.nationalcatholicreporter.org/todaystake/tt082803. htm.

30. Quoted in Lidia Hunter, "Plan for Inter-Ocean Canal Reborn," Inside Costa Rica, September 14, 2003. http://in sidecostarica.com/specialreports/nicaragua_plan_for_ canal_reborn.htm.

31. Paul Jeffrey, "When Agriculture and Ecology Compete: The Struggle to Protect Nicaragua's Wilderness," *New World Outlook*, September/October 2001. http://gbgm-umc.org/nwo/01so/nicaragua.html#reform.

32. Quoted in *Economist*, "Waiting for the Fat Man to Sing; Corruption in Latin America," August 24, 2002.

GLOSSARY

Black Caribs: Descendants of black Caribbean slaves who migrated to Nicaragua from Britain's Caribbean settlements.

buccaneers: British pirates who carried out raids against Spanish ships and settlements during colonial times.

cloud rain forest: A rain forest that grows in the mist at altitudes above about 3,000 feet (914m).

compadrazgo: A common practice in Nicaragua in which parents choose godparents to help support their children.

Contras: A group of guerrilla fighters financed by the United States during the 1980s to attack and bring down the Sandinista government in Nicaragua.

costeño: A term used to refer to minority populations of ethnic Nicaraguans living in the Caribbean region of the country.

FSLN: The Frente Sandinista de Liberación Nacional, or Sandinista National Liberation Front, a group that opposed the Somoza regime in Nicaragua; also called the Sandinistas.

Garifuna: A group of Black Caribs in eastern Nicaragua who have a mixed West Indian and African ancestry.

guerrilla war: A type of unconventional war technique in which small groups of fighters harass, sabotage, or stage attacks and then fade back into the population, making detection and counterattack difficult.

International Monetary Fund (IMF): An international organization set up in 1944 to stabilize economies and promote world trade by lending money to developing nations.

machismo: An attitude of exagerrated masculinity.

mestizo: Nicaraguans of mixed Spanish and Indian blood.

Miskito Indians: An indigenous tribe from Nicaragua's Caribbean coast region whose ancestors include people who migrated from Colombia and black Caribbean slaves who fled to Nicaragua from Britain's Caribbean settlements.

Mosquito Coast: A humid, low-lying, coastal area on Nicaragua's eastern side bordering the Caribbean Sea.

Navidad: The term for Christmas in Nicaragua.

Nica: The nickname Nicaraguans from western Nicaragua use to refer to themselves.

Pascua: The term for Easter in Nicaragua.

Purísima: The Immaculate Conception of the Virgin Mary, a holiday celebrated in Nicaragua on December 8.

Sandinistas: A group that opposed the Somoza regime in Nicaragua also called the Sandinista National Liberation Front.

tierra caliente: Coastal areas of Nicaragua known as "hot lands" where temperatures average between 70 and 90 degrees Fahrenheit (21 to 32 degrees Celsius).

tierra fría: Higher mountain elevations of Nicaragua known as "cold lands" where temperatures average between 50 and 70 degrees Fahrenheit (10 to 21 degrees Celsius).

tierra templada: Areas in the central highlands of Nicaragua known as "temperate lands" where temperatures range between 60 and 80 degrees Fahrenheit (15 to 26 degrees Celsius).

UNO: The Unión Nacional Opositora, or National Opposition Union, a coalition party led by conservative Violeta Chamorro and backed by the United States in the 1990 Nicaraguan elections.

World Bank: An international bank set up in the 1940s to provide loans and economic advice to developing countries.

CHRONOLOGY

1502
Nicaragua is discovered by Spain when Christopher Columbus arrives on the Caribbean side.

1522
Spanish explorer Gil González Dávila names Nicaragua after a local Indian chief, Nicarao.

1523–1524
Spanish settlements are established at León and Granada.

1660s–1700s
British explorers establish settlements on Nicaragua's Caribbean coast.

1700s
Black Caribs, people of mixed black and Indian ancestry from the Carib tribe of the British West Indies, arrive on Nicaragua's Caribbean coast.

1821
Nicaragua declares its independence from Spain.

1823
Nicaragua joins Costa Rica, El Salvador, Guatemala, and Honduras as part of a federation called the United Provinces of Central America.

1838
Nicaragua becomes fully independent, but Britain and the United States soon become involved in Nicaraguan politics and affairs.

1855
American William Walker seizes control of the government of Nicaragua.

1893
General José Santos Zelaya, a Liberal, seizes power and establishes a dictatorship.

1909
U.S. marines help overthrow Zelaya.

1912
The United States again sends troops to Nicaragua to maintain order; they remain there until 1933.

1927–1933
Guerrillas led by rebel Augusto César Sandino fight against the U.S. military presence in Nicaragua.

1933
U.S. marines are withdrawn from Nicaragua, and Sandino agrees to lay down his arms.

1934
Sandino is assassinated on the orders of the National Guard commander, General Anastasio Somoza García.

1937
General Somoza is elected president, beginning a forty-three-year dictatorship by his family.

1956
General Somoza is assassinated, but is succeeded as president by his son Luís Somoza Debayle.

1961
The Sandinista National Liberation Front (FSLN) is founded to fight the Somoza dictatorship.

1967
Luís Somoza dies and is succeeded as president by his brother, Anastasio Somoza.

1978
The assassination of the leader of the opposition Democratic Liberation Union, Pedro Joaquín Chamorro, triggers a general strike and brings moderates and the FSLN together against Somoza.

1979
After an FSLN military offensive, Somoza resigns effective July 17. The FSLN guerrillas (the Sandinistas) take control of the Nicaraguan government.

1980

The FSLN government, led by Daniel Ortega, begins a series of social reforms.

1981–1982

The United States cuts off aid to Nicaragua and provides
support to Contra rebels who stage attacks on the Sandinista government.

1984

Nicaragua holds its first democratic elections; Daniel Ortega is elected president.

1985

The United States imposes a total trade embargo on
Nicaragua.

1987

Nicaragua adopts a new constitution that provides for a democratic government. Nicaragua signs a peace agreement
negotiated by Costa Rican president Oscar Arias Sánchez.

1988

Hurricane Joan hits Nicaragua, causing great damage.

1990

The U.S.-backed National Opposition Union (UNO) defeats
the FSLN in elections and Violeta Chamorro becomes president.

1996

Liberal Party candidate Arnoldo Alemán is elected president.

2001

Liberal Party candidate Enrique Bolaños is elected president.

2002

Former president Alemán is charged with money laundering and embezzlement during his term in office.

2003

Alemán is jailed for twenty years for corruption.

2004

Under agreements negotiated by the International Monetary Fund and the World Bank, 73 percent of Nicaragua's international debt is forgiven.

For Further Reading

Books

K. Melissa Cerar, *Teenage Refugees from Nicaragua Speak Out.* New York: Rosen, 1995. First-person accounts from teen refugees are placed in the context of the political unrest of Nicaragua.

Luis Garay, *The Kite.* Plattsburgh, NY: Tundra, 2002. A young adult book of fiction that follows the life of a poor, young Nicaraguan boy.

Marion Morrison, *Nicaragua: Enchantment of the World.* New York: Children's Press, 2002. A young adult book that provides an overview of Nicaragua, including geography, history, government, economy, culture, religion, and many other topics.

Janet Riehecky, *Nicaragua.* Mankato, MN: Bridgestone, 2002. An easy-to-read introduction to the geography, animals, food, and culture of Nicaragua.

Web Sites

Lonely Planet (www.lonelyplanet.com/destinations/central_america/nicaragua/index.htm). A travel Web site that contains useful information about various aspects of life and travel in Nicaragua, including discussions of the country's history, culture, and environment.

UNICEF (www.unicef.org/infobycountry/nicaragua_24060.html). A site run by an international aid agency that describes the life of a fifteen-year-old girl from Nicaragua and provides some information about the education system in the country.

U.S. Department of State (http://travel.state.gov/travel/ nicaragua.html). A U.S. government Web site providing practical information and travel warnings for people who plan to visit Nicaragua.

The World Factbook: Nicaragua (www.cia.gov/cia/public ations/ factbook/geos/nu.html). This U.S. government site gives geographical, political, economic, and other information on Nicaragua.

WORKS CONSULTED

BOOKS

David Close, *Nicaragua: Politics, Economics, and Society.* New York: Pinter, 1988. A scholarly discussion of Nicaragua's history, society, economy, political system, and public policies while under Sandinista leadership.

Paul Glassman, *Nicaragua Guide: Spectacular and Unspoiled.* Champlain, NY: Travel Line, 1996. A travel guide to Nicaragua containing short descriptions of Nicaragua's history, society, climate, and culture.

Nathan A. Haverstock and John P. Hoover, *Nicaragua in Pictures.* New York: Sterling, 1974. A useful overview of Nicaragua's geography, history, government, people, and economy, illustrated with black-and-white photos.

Katherine Isbester, *Still Fighting: The Nicaraguan Women's Movement, 1977–2000.* Pittsburgh, PA: University of Pittsburgh Press, 2001. A scholarly analysis of the formation and dynamics of the Nicaraguan women's movement from the time of the Sandinista revolution to the year 2000.

Tim L. Merrill, ed., *Nicaragua: A Country Study.* Washington, DC: U.S. Government Printing Office, 1994. A Library of Congress report on Nicaragua that provides a good overview of its history, society, economy, government, military, and foreign policy.

Hazel Plunkett, *Nicaragua: A Guide to the People, Politics, and Culture.* New York: Interlink 1999. An authoritative and up-to-date guide to Nicaragua's history, politics, economy, environment, people, and culture.

Thomas W. Walker, *Nicaragua: The Land of Sandino*, third edition. Boulder, CO: Westview, 1991. An understandable yet scholarly overview of Nicaragua's history, economy, culture, and government.

PERIODICALS

Rose Marie Berger and Brian Bolton, "Sweeping Up Corruption," *Sojourners*, May 2004.

Economist, "In the Shadow of the Caudillos; Nicaragua's Besieged President," November 13, 2004.

———, "Waiting for the Fat Man to Sing; Corruption in Latin America," August 24, 2002.

Gretchen Gundrum, "Trying to Do Justice," *America*, January 21, 2002.

Latin Trade, "The Future Is Now," March 2003.

Tim Rogers, "Good News on the Air," *Latin Trade*, June 2004.

INTERNET SOURCES

Filadelfo Aleman, "IMF, World Bank Forgives Nicaragua's Debt," January 23, 2004. www.belleville.com/mld/belle ville/business/7781797.htm.

Cristiana Chamorro Barrios, "The Challenges for Radio Ya and Radio Corporación," *Pulsa del Periodismo*, 2000. www.pulso.org/English/Archives/Nicaragua.htm.

BBC News, "Country Profile: Nicaragua," August 20, 2004. http://news.bbc.co.uk/1/hi/world/americas/country_pro files/1225218.stm.

———, "Timeline: Nicaragua," December 30, 2004. http://news.bbc.co.uk/1/hi/world/americas/country_pro files/1225283.stm.

Bensenville Community Public Library, "Nicaragua-Culture Overview," 2000–2002. http://expedition.bensenville.lib. il.us/CentralAmerica/Nicaragua/Culture.htm.

Joshua Berman and Randy Wood, "Nicaragua: Why So Many Travelers Are Discovering This 'Black Sheep of Central

America,'" Moon Handbooks, January 25, 2003. www.
gonomad.com/market/0301/nicaraguaguide.html.

Bureau of Democracy, Human Rights, and Labor,
"Nicaragua: Country Reports on Human Rights Prac-
tices—2002," March 31, 2003. www.state.gov/g/drl/rls/
hrrpt/2002/18339.htm.

Matthew Creelman, "Central America: Land Reform Put
Off," *Latinamerica Press*, February 28, 2000. www.rtf
cam.org/report/volume_20/No_2/article_9.htm.

Dennis Martinez Foundation, "Hurricane Mitch," 2001.
www.dennismartinezfoundation.org/pro_mitch.html.

Jay Feldman, "Baseball in Nicaragua," *Whole Earth Review*,
Fall 1987. www.findarticles.com/p/articles/mi_m1510/
is_1987_Fall/ai_5151507.

Folk Art and Craft Exchange, "Nicaraguan Pottery." www.
folkart.com/nims.

Tom Fox, "Living Nicaragua's Dubious Distinction," *National
Catholic Reporter*, August 28, 2003. www.nationalcatholic
reporter.org/todaystake/tt082803.htm.

Lidia Hunter, "Plan for Inter-Ocean Canal Reborn," Inside
Costa Rica, September 14, 2003. http://insidecostarica.
com/specialreports/nicaragua_plan_for_canal_reborn.
htm.

International Monetary Fund, "IMF and World Bank Support US$4.5 Billion in Debt Service Relief for Nicaragua,"
January 23, 2004. www.imf.org/external/np/sec/pr/2004/
pr0411.htm.

———, "Nicaragua: Fourth Review Under the Three-Year
Arrangement Under the Poverty Reduction and Growth
Facility," March 18, 2004. www.imf.org/external/pubs/
cat/longres.cfm?sk=17265.0.

Paul Jeffrey, "When Agriculture and Ecology Compete: The
Struggle to Protect Nicaragua's Wilderness," *New World
Outlook*, September/October 2001. http://gbgm-umc.
org/nwo/01so/nicaragua.html#reform.

Lidiana, "Immaculate Conception/La Purisima—Nicaragua," KidLink, December 8, 1996. www.kidlink.org/KIDPROJ/MCC/mcc0338.html.

Wilmor López, "Celebrating Life: Las Fiestas de San Jerónimo," Nicaragua's Best Guide. www.guideofnicaragua.com/1202/JeronimoEN.html.

MSN *Encarta*, "Nicaragua," 2004. http://encarta.msn.com/encyclopedia_761577584_3/Nicaragua.html.

Rodolfo Narváez, "Celebrating Life: The Bull-Deer Dance," Nicaragua's Best Guide. www.guideofnicaragua.com/Octubre/CelebratingToroVenado.html.

Nicaragua Network Environmental Committee, "Nicaragua's Proposed Dry Canal," n.d. http://environment.nicanet.org/dry_canal2.htm.

———, "Protecting Nicaragua's Forests," n.d. http://environment.nicanet.org/forests.htm.

PageWise, "Lago de Nicaragua," 2002. http://nd.essortment.com/lagodenicaragu_rbxb.htm.

Claudia Paguaga, "Enrique Bolaños Geyer: A Step Towards Consolidating Democracy in Nicaragua," February 2002, Revista INTER-FORUM. www.revistainterforum.com/english/articles/032502artprin_en.html.

Marcela Sanchez, "Crucifying Nicaragua's Redeemer," *Washington Post*, December 9, 2004. www.washingtonpost.com/wp-dyn/articles/A52649-2004Dec9.html.

Shark Gallery, "Bull Shark," n.d. http://shark-gallery.netfirms.com/med/bull.htm.

Spartacus, "Augusto Sandino," n.d. www.spartacus.schoolnet.co.uk/COLDsandino.htm.

———, "Daniel Ortega," n.d. www.spartacus.schoolnet.co.uk/COLDortega.htm.

Wikipedia, "Music of Nicaragua," n.d. www.searchspaniel.com/index.php/Music_of_Nicaragua.

World Bank Group, "Poverty Declines in Nicaragua from 1993–2001," June 2, 2004. http://web.worldbank.org/WB SITE/EXTERNAL/COUNTRIES/LACEXT/NICARAGUAEXTN/ 0,,contentMDK:20208067~menuPK:258694~pagePK:1411 37~piPK:141127~theSitePK:258689,00.html.

Yahoo! Travel, "León, Nicaragua: Overview," 2005. http:// travel.yahoo.com/p-travelguide-782346-leon_leon-i.

INDEX

Picture Credits

ABOUT THE AUTHOR

Debra A. Miller is a writer and lawyer with a passion for current events and history. She began her law career in Washington, D.C., where she worked on legislative, policy, and legal matters in government, public interest, and private law firm positions. She now lives with her husband in Encinitas, California. She has written and edited publications for legal publishers, as well as numerous books and anthologies on historical and political topics.